Ken Bruen was born in Ga
sixteen novels, he spent twe
teacher in Africa, Japan, South East Asia and South America. He now lives in Galway City with his wife and daughter. Serpent's Tail also publish *Rilke on Black.*

Praise for *Her Last Call to Louis MacNeice*

'Very nasty, very funny' *Big Issue*

'If this thriller was any more hard-boiled you'd be able to paint a face on it and roll it down the hill… Noir at its grungiest' *Good Book Guide*

'Fast-paced, tough and explosive – you may need a calming bromide standing by' *Irish Times*

Also by Ken Bruen and published by Serpent's Tail

Rilke on Black

'The most startlingly original crime novel to emerge this decade' *GQ*

'The reading equivalent of a boxer's sharp jab to the solar plexus. It's fast-paced, tough, and pretty sexy' *Pulp*

'Boiled harder than salad eggs and much more likely to leave a nasty taste in your mouth' *Big Issue*

Her Last Call to Louis MacNeice

Ken Bruen

To John L. Williams

A complete catalogue record for this book can
be obtained from the British Library on request

First published in 1998 by Serpent's Tail,
4 Blackstock Mews, London N4 2BT
website: www.serpentstail.com

First published in this 5-star edition in 2005

Printed by Mackays of Chatham, plc

10 9 8 7 6 5 4 3 2 1

PROLOGUE

The blast took her face off. Two seconds of pressure on the trigger and a full shotgun load went roaring out.

We'd been doing good. In with a maximum of ferocity. Get 'em terrorised, shouting 'Get the fuck down – NOW.'

Push push push.

Let 'em see the guns, hear the manic screaming of very dangerous men.

Doc had planted devices at the

cop shop
Tesco
The Masonic Lodge

They'd gone off like lubrication. You had the noise, smoke, confusion and then we're in – 'MENACE' writ brutal large.

Oh yeah, fuckin' A.

Bingo, the motherload. More cash than Camelot, two bin-liners overflowing with readies.

Everything hunky-dory. . . . and then . . .

Then I shot the cashier in the face.

I guess it began with Cassie.

The cop stopped me on Kennington Road. I was having a bad day. As if a neon sign above my head, high-lit to read

'FUCK WITH THIS GUY'

They'd seen it.

I turned off the engine and waited. A sign of middle age when policemen look young. This one looked ten and had seen too many cop shows. He had the saunter and the cap adjustment. Get that sucker on to look mean. He wasn't wearing shades but he wanted to . . . and badly. I expected him to drawl in a Kentucky twang . . . 'assume the position' or, at the very least, 'what we got here Bubba?' What he did say was, 'Do you know why I stopped you?'

I'd no idea as I hadn't been speeding and the car was in good nick. Tax, insurance, all that good shit was in order. So, I went for it.

''Cos you're a bad bastard.'

My parents were hard-line Presbyterian. Wouldn't make love standing up lest people thought they were dancing. Fun was indeed the F-word. They were a potent mix, she was from Belfast and he from Glasgow. Settling in London, they brought little as baggage save bitterness. My old man kept pigeons, jeez . . . I hate them. As a child I feared heights but feared him more. The birds he kept on the roof. Our house was a three-storey one in Battersea, near the power station. The yellow light came creepin' each evening. Course, that was the time he liked to feed the birds. He'd haul me up there, the yellow light like sickness on my bare legs, fear like regularity in my stomach.

When I was fourteen, I started to grow. An October evening, he'd bullied me as usual on the roof. The cooing of the pigeons as nauseating as cowardice. He was saying, 'What did I tell you boy, feed them slow. Don't you listen.'

And I said, 'Feed them yourself.'

All sorts of shit the Presbyterians can't get a handle on but leading the field is disobedience. He'd grabbed me by the scruff and hauled me to the edge of the roof, roarin' 'Better you should throw yourself to the concrete than fly in the face of your father.'

Through the years I've re-played, re-said that scene. I'd like to think it was courage or even anger that forced my answer. Mainly, I believe, the words came from my South-East London education. The streets in all their glory rushing up through my chest to explode 'Fuck you.'

And he'd clutched at his chest. I've since learnt the word 'apoplexy', and wow, he got to live it then. Can a face go purple, his sure tried and he toppled over, finally experiencing a moment of flight. Sometimes in dreams, I've seen me push him and I know my mother was convinced that I did. When I wake, I don't feel guilty. Well, the cop had a similar expression but before he could respond, a car came tearing out of the estates, burned rubber at the kerb, and shot off towards the Oval. Two pandas came screeching in pursuit and the cop's radio blared into static. He shouted into it, 'Responding . . . responding.'

He gave me the look, said, 'Your lucky day but I'll be watching for you. . . .'

As he started to pull away, I said, 'I'll miss you.'

It was that day I met Cassie. On the Walworth Road, I nipped into Marks and Spencers, got some groceries. Time back, Elvis Costello had a song called 'Watching the

Detectives'. I like to do that, see how a real asshole makes a living. I spotted the store's plainclothes operator near the frozen meat. Which is a fairly apt metaphor . . . and . . . he was clocking somebody.

A woman in her thirties, pushing a trolley. Wearing jeans, sweatshirt, Reeboks . . . *pink* Reeboks and new. Lookin' comfortable. She had the moves, like Mary Tyler Moore, the expression. Remember the opening sequence to that show? She picks up a steak, glances at it, near grimaces and chucks it back in the freezer. I loved that, wanted to marry her right then, I was eleven.

She looked like Sarah Miles . . . or how she used to. Remember, with Dirk Bogarde in *The Servant* . . . or *Ryan's Daughter*. Before she went ape. It's the closest the English get to Style. Class is something else, they figure they invented it. She had a loose long coat and you knew it had them big vacuum pockets, only one reason you wear that. But she was quick, I'll give her that. The package went inside there about as fast as it gets. Not fast enough. A surge of electricity went through the store detective. Time to move. I walked up to her, said, 'Put it back, you've been spotted.'

The shock on her face was mega. I kept going and the detective moved after me. Reached me as I got to the door, said, 'Don't think I don't know what you did, I'd have had her bang to rights.'

He must have been all of twenty-five and, to judge by his eyes, all of them miserable. I asked, 'Spoil yer day, did I?'

'I'll remember you, see if I don't.'

'Jeez, everybody's saying that.'

Not sure how to proceed, he raised his voice: 'Is that all you've to say for yerself?'

'No . . . I have more.'

'Oh yeah?'

'Yeah . . . fuck off.'

When she emerged, I was sitting on the bench outside. She stopped, looked quizzical, asked, 'Why are you waiting. You've no authority out here.'

Yank.

'You got that right sister, authority was never one of my assets but I'm not a store detective, just a punter.'

Understanding lit her face . . . then something else . . . like shame maybe. A horrendous sight.

'You saved me.'

'Well. . . .'

'How can I thank you . . . oh GAWD . . . I'm so embarrassed . . . I get spasms . . . I . . .'

'Wanna eat?'

'Excuse me?'

I stood up, explained, 'It's not a difficult question . . . but lemme break it down. A: Are you hungry. B: If so, lemme treat you. A new joint has opened down the road . . . What do you say?'

She appeared to give it serious thought, said, 'Okey-dokey, how could I turn down an offer like that.'

It looked like the place had just opened, like in the previous five minutes. We sat at a table, admired the unfinished surroundings. A guy built to bounce came over, he had the dazed look of a drinker. Everything about him was big but not muscle, flabbiness. A line of grey sweat nibbled at his temples and upper lip. He'd a bright plastic name tag which read 'Hi, I'm Bert.'

He didn't appear pleased to see us. But it wasn't personal. He'd had a bad day in his past and was holding on to it . . . and grimly. I asked, 'Are you Bert?'

'Who's asking.'

'Jeez, take it easy, if you're hiding out, you've picked the wrong disguise.'

The woman said, 'Bert, how about you bring us some

coffee . . . then we'll chow down. Give us all a minute to consider the words of Desiderata.'

'Wha?'

'Coffee Bert . . . two coffees . . . Before Tuesday . . . OK.'

He rumbled off.

She smiled, said, 'My hunch is he's also the short-order chef so cancel them burgers.'

'Yeah . . . you're American.'

'That a disappointment?'

'No . . . I mean . . . it's fine. I like yer accent, it's just . . . surprising.'

'You didn't know Americans were shoplifters.'

'Not that, what I didn't know was Americans were *bad* shoplifters.'

And she laughed. The kind you never expect a woman to have, deep and downright bawdy. Where she goes all the way with it and doesn't give a toss how she appears. A real whack-it-for-all-its-worth job. I liked that a whole lot. She asked, 'So . . . my hero, my saviour, you got a name, we've already established you've got balls, yeah, ask Bert . . . See if I'm wrong?'

A woman uses words like that to you . . . you're usually paying for the service. I said, 'It's Cooper.'

'That's it . . . you were born at High Noon?'

'Very snappy . . . with wit like that, you're wasted in Marks and Spencers . . . and what's your name?'

'Cassie.'

'Short for Cassandra . . . yeah? So, they call you Cass.'

She rummaged in her coat, took out a crumpled soft pack of Camel Lights, shook one free and using a matchbook, lit up, dragged deep . . . said, 'You're hard of hearing? Or is it an English thing? My name is Cassie, you got that?'

'Jeez, over and out, bit testy are you. You'd love my mate, the Doc.'

'He's a doctor?'

'Doc Marten . . . he's a villain, thing is . . . he wears Docs, always did and long before they became a fashion accessory. The traditional black-laced jobs, with steel hubs and tops. Built for kicking . . . and hard.'

The coffee came, it looked a little like the ketchup and Bert slapped a bill down. I said, 'Hope you included service.'

He grunted.

She said, 'Louis MacNeice's mother died when he was seven.'

I didn't know how much grief she'd anticipated.

'Jeez, tough break. I guess I'd be more broke up if I knew who he was.'

'Don't look now but Bert is shooting the bird.'

'He's what?'

'It's an obscene gesture, don't you guys speak English?'

'Sure . . . and if you stick around you'll learn some.'

'My mother died when I was seven, so Louis and I are spiritually connected. Wanna drink?'

I looked at the bill, said, 'Five friggin' quid, dream on sucker.'

I left a pound on the table and we went outside. I could see Bert through the plate glass window reading the writing on the table. Time he read the writing on the wall. Cassie asked, 'Can you run?'

'Wot?'

And she took the ketchup bottle from the coat, shouted, 'It's a goddamn homer.'

I could hear the glass shatter as we tore across the road. We reached my car, she asked, 'This is yours.'

'Sure is.'

'Can I drive?'

I gave her the look, said in what I considered a passable twang, 'In your language . . . Get real.'

We got in and she sank in her seat, she gave a low whistle, said, 'Way to go.'

It's an impressive car, least I think so. A Subaru Impreza, its cousin won the Monte Carlo rally. Yeah, like that. Lemme break it down, it's turbo charged, two litre, four wheel drive. It's got bonnet scoop, vents, bumper air intakes, and these mother driving lamps. On the up and up, it goes for near twenty grand. As I hit the ignition, she asked, 'It looks like it's cookin', but is it all flash?'

'Listen lady, how many cars will hit 30 mph from go in two seconds and show 60 in six before rushing on past 140.'

She gave a low chuckle, mean and nasty.

'And go right to sleep after.'

I ignored her, manoeuvred past the roundabout at the Elephant and Castle, headed for the Oval. Cassie turned her head, listening attentively.

She said, 'I hear Morocco, the wail of the minaret, the call to prayer.'

I wondered had I taken a wrong turn in the conversation. Between passing into third gear had I missed something. Asked, 'Did I miss something?'

'An automobile like this, with a sexy name, seems a goddamn waste in the city, I mean do you get to hit 100-plus often?'

She had a point, a fairly irritating one but nonetheless . . . I said, 'It does the job.'

'So would a pushbike.'

Before I could sulk she asked, 'What's a gal gotta do to get a drink?'

'We're near my place, want to go there?'

'Gets my vote.'

I live in Meadow Road. About an umpire from the Oval

Cricket Ground. On the outside, it looks ordinary, one up, one down.

Like that.

The money was spent inside. It's a little flash but hey, I liked to think I had some moves. I turned the engine off, got out and went round to hold her door. She went Southern belle, drawled, 'My, my, my . . . y'all a gentleman Ashley.'

'Whatever.'

Inside, I led her down the hall and stood back. Let the house do its number. Remote control panels to do near all save shout hello. Cost me a fortune and half that again. She stood in the living room, said, 'Holy shit, who lives here.'

I hit the remote and the bar glided up.

'A drink?'

'Got any Bourbon?'

'I got Scotch.'

'Scotch's good, on the rocks, beer chaser.'

I did that, handed them to her, took a large hit of my own. Yeah, that was it, said, 'Sit down.'

She did, unlaced her Reeboks, kicked 'em off, curled her feet under her. How do women do that or, more's the point, why. It looks uncomfortable but she seemed happy with it, asked, 'So who'd you kill for this?'

I thought I'd let that slide for a bit, see how it shaped, so I asked her, 'What's a Yank doing shoplifting in South-East London? I mean, wouldn't Harrods or Selfridges be more appropriate.'

'I'm hoping to take my Ph.D. in Metaphysics.'

'What shop does them?'

She gave a toss of her head.

'Don't be a horse's ass. Ontology is the primary element in metaphysics, you know that I guess.'

'On . . . wot?'

'It's the ontological dilemma. What really exists as opposed to that which appears to exist but does not.'

'I appear to have lost you.'

'Gimme another shot of that Scotch.'

I did and asked,

'OK, so let's say you grab this Ph.D. – it qualifies you to do what?'

She shrugged, it caused her breasts to move forward and I felt something move myself.

'Oh I guess I'll probably still be stealing but at least I'll be able to look into the soul of the store detective.'

'Shit, don't bother. I already did and it's a wilderness. Not a place you'd want to visit.'

'Very deep Cooper. Tell me, are you a winner?'

'Fuck knows, depends who's keeping score.'

'I'm serious here guy. I don't want to know from losers, you gettin' this. I've been nickled and dimed to death.'

'Hey . . . lady, get a grip, look around you, am I hurting here?'

'What . . . this proves what exactly. That your taste is way up your ass . . . and an automobile that ain't worth shit in the city.'

That was about it, I'd had it. Put down my glass, time to fold her tent. But she stood, came to me, said, 'Fuck me rough.'

Before I could reply, she put her hand on my crotch, pulled the zip down, took a grip of the action. She purred, 'Oh you're ready to pop.'

I was . . . and in a little while, I did. She was sitting astride me and gave a slow smile, said, 'I've a piece of you now, you'll never ball any other broad . . . you hear me?'

'What's this . . . post-coital aggression?'

'It's the truth, remember you've been warned.'

I didn't know how to answer this so I didn't. She rolled

offa me, said, 'You grab some Zzzzz's and I'll wake you with a blow job. You'll come to, so to speak. Sound good?'

Yeah, well it didn't sound too bad so I grabbed the shut-eye. Dreamt too, of pigeons and breaking glass and store detectives shouting 'It's a fair cop.' Bert was there too but I don't really recall what he was doing, save sweating.

When I woke, she was gone. Was I disappointed. Well, my body wanted her but my head roared THANK FUCK FOR THAT.

A note was propped on the coffee table. Not a note, a bloody manuscript. Jeez, maybe she'd left me her thesis and how long had I slept. Checked my watch, I'd been out four hours . . . What? The note consisted of long manuscript pages. I read the first.

Hi lover,
You'll have slept well. Certainly you'll have slept long as I added a little something to your drink. I felt you were a tad tense, as you English might say. You'll find it left you parched so I only drank half your juice.

She was right, I went and got the OJ . . . swamped it. Read on:

Took me ages to locate the goddamn phone but I guess we both know I already have your number. In my rummaging, I found a sawn-off shotgun and an automatic pistol. How dangerous is this neighbourhood? I confiscated them. Just kidding big guy . . . lighten up, these are the jokes. And I also discovered boxes of money. Naturally, I skimmed some bills off the top 'cos it's what I do.

I've put down some Louis MacNeice as your education begins NOW. Pay attention, I'll be asking questions . . . and WHERE ARE THOSE ESSAYS! Can you smell me offa you . . . you're all over me you stallion, you well-hung colossus.

Whoops, here's my cab. Hate to heat and run but . . . later . . . yeah,

Your Cassie

'Fuck me,' I said.

Went to check the wardrobes and sure enough, the shoe boxes were open, she'd helped herself to a very generous wedge (of bills). The pistol was gone. So now the bitch was armed. I already knew she was dangerous.

Made some strong coffee and had a shower. Took a hard look at myself in the full-length mirror and didn't relish what I saw. Sandy hair already thinning out, hooded brown eyes and a poor nose. My mouth was like a thin compressed line and even in laughter, it didn't improve a whole amount. Deep ridges down the side of my nose as if they'd been cut. But I had good teeth and worked at keeping them. I was five feet ten inches tall and had exercised for a lotta years. The muscle still held but it was loosening. A pot belly was beginning to shape and fuck, nothing could impede its progress . . . lest I stop eating . . . yeah. The booze didn't help but I wasn't about to get that concerned. Did Jack Nicholson care?

I dressed in old Levi cords, so faded they could have got a pension and wow, were they comfortable or what. One more wash, you know, they were history . . . *sayonara* and good night.

I pulled on a hooded black sweatshirt, to accessorize my hooded eyes, it read 'I'M A GAS'. Yeah, just couldn't stem the humour, I was a real fuckin' comedian.

Completed the outfit with a pair of battered moccasins that whispered, 'I love your feet . . . I love you.'
Sure felt like it. Put some gel in my hair to get that wet look. When you're forty-two years old, you'll try any

gimmick. It made my hair look wet which I guess is the point. I hoped for that crumpled Don Johnson effect but I got close-call wino. Tried that American voice again, roared ENOUGH ALREADY! And went to read the MacNeice piece.

'Without heroics, without belief
I send you, as I am not rich
Nothing but odds and ends a thief
bundled up in the last ditch
for few are able to keep moving
they drag and flag in the traffic
while you are alive beyond question
like the dazzle on the sea my darling.'

Hey! Are you getting this? Here's some more purely as introduction.

'The bullfight, the fanderillas like
Christmas candles
And the scrawled hammer and sickle
It was all copy – impenetrable surface
I did not look for the sneer beneath the surface
Why should I trouble, an addict to oblivion
Running away from the Gods of my own hearth
With no intention
Of finding Gods elsewhere.'

You don't get it Cooper do you . . . I know you don't but, by Christ, you will. Here endeth the lesson, memorise the underlined pieces. Auden gave some lines to MacNeice, I think they had you in mind. I'll sign off with them.

'Shall I drink your health before
The gun-butt raps upon the door.'

I put down the sheets, drained the coffee and said, 'Memorise! Kiss my ass.'

The Doc was saying, 'I keep breaking out in spots . . . spots like Croydon, Norwood, and bloody Brixton.'

The pub was packed and he was in full flight. What they call a two-fisted drinker and he drank in a similar fashion. A big man, six feet two inches, near 240 pounds and a lot of it was muscle. He kept his head shaved to the skull and it all added to his bull appearance. But startlingly blue eyes, a broken nose and full mouth. He was dressed in a white tracksuit and of course, the Doc Martens, polished to a frenzied spit. I met him in prison, he'd been in and out of Pentonville more times than the postman. I'd been convicted of GBH . . . which was OK . . . if they wanted to call it grievous bodily harm, I wasn't arguing the toss. A mugger had hopped on my back down in Waterloo and I'd tried to kill the fucker. In fact, I was sure I had done as I gave it my best shot. I hadn't done good in the nick, I couldn't get the rhythm . . . and would you want to. In fights all the time, I could learn the words but I couldn't catch the melody. That's when I met the Doc and he showed me the score. Why a huge Irishman became my solution is one of those odd events that defy analysis. Our friendship continued in the straight world and we went into business together.

He'd taken advantage of the Open University to attain his 'O' Levels and went all the way through to take a B.A. in Literature. It demonstrated, he said, not so much how smart he was as the length of time he'd been inside. I reckoned if anyone knew the MacNeice dude, it was him. Our business brought in a lotta cash but fuck, he needed it. The man loved to spend.

This evening, he'd thrown an impromptu party in our local as his team had bought a new player. Fuck knows, they needed to. What he'd done was put a grand behind the bar and ya-hoo, it was open season . . . party time. He'd once said to me, 'They don't trust an educated Irishman, it's like an uppity nigger.'

I said, 'As maybe! But they get downright paranoid with a flash one even more. Do you have to be so blatant with the cash? I mean I've heard of conspicuous consumption but this is friggin' rubbin' their noses in it.'

'Ah Cooper, me oul segotia, you worry too much. You can't take it with you.'

'Yeah, but you're hell bent on letting every other bastard take it with him.'

'You're a miserable sod, why are the English so cautious?'

''Cos we have to deal with you flamin' paddies is why. We'll have to pull another job sooner than planned.'

I caught his eye, signalled the corner booth, our office of sorts. Wading through the crowd, he was pumping hands, yelling hello, home is the fuckin' hero. His face was awash in sweat and his eyes alight. Threw an arm round me, asked, 'How's it cutting, yah worry guts?'

'Sit down Doc, I need to talk.'

'Uh-uh, you got a girl in trouble?'

'Just listen OK, can you fuckin' do that, take five minutes off from the hearty hail-fuck-well-met, can you.'

It lashed him, his eyes lost their light a moment, as if a candle had been blown out, I said, 'Sorry, I didn't mean that but I need your undivided.'

He sat down, took out a hankie, with his team colours, mopped his face, said, 'Oh you meant it alright. But sometimes I'm afraid if I stop, I'll never get motoring again, I keep bein' afraid I'll miss something. Anyway, fire away.'

I gave him a rundown on the day, covered near all. He looked into my face, asked, 'Did you give her one?'

'What?'

'Did you ride her?'

'Good Lord, why don't you just come right out and ask me . . . why beat about the bush?'

'Sounds like you beat around the old bush. So . . . did you do the business, give her a rub of the relic.'

'Em . . . in a manner of speaking.'

He gave a huge laugh, threw back his head and went with it. Ever see or hear Dyan Cannon laugh? Yeah . . . the whole shebang, light on a dark street, like that.

'Aw Jaysus Coop, you'll kill me. The English are a race apart, what d'ya do, talk dirty to her.'

'OK . . . OK . . . so . . . we had intercourse.'

'Intercourse, what . . .? By the Lord Harry did ye study first . . . what goes where . . . after you dear . . . no, no . . . I insist . . . put it where you desire. No wonder ye like *Carry On* pictures.'

'You're a big help Doc.'

'And lifted the pistol did she, the heathen bitch . . . bit careless were you?'

'Hey, she slipped me a Mickey Finn.'

'And you slipped her . . . OK . . . sorry.'

'Have you heard of MacNeice then?'

Doc had done the English piss-take in a haughty law-di-daw. Now he switched to what I'd heard him call his West-Brit accent.

'I come from an island, Ireland, a nation built upon violence and morose vendettas. My diehard countrymen like drayhorses, drag their ruin behind them, shooting straight in the cause of crooked thinking. Their greed is sugared with pretence of public spirit, from all of which I am an exile.'

I didn't know was this Doc or MacNeice till he said, 'He was like me, said,

"In short we must keep moving
to keep pace
or else drop into limbo
the dead place." '

I threw up my hands.

'What the fuck is this, everyone's doing recitations, did I miss something. Who is this fuck.'

'Take it easy Coop, I also do Yeats . . . how about a nice bit of Browning?'

'Fuck off.'

''Course you crowd adore Rupert Brooke, all that romantic dying and heroism with a hint of buggery:

"And some corner of a foreign field
shall be forever England"

Yeah, well he got his wish, they bloody buried him in it. Let's get a drink, I'm parched.'

Back to the bar and ordered double Scotches. Got on the other side of them, I said, 'What should I do?'

'Get shot of her.'

'That's it . . . for this I sat through poetry at eleven.'

'Look Coop, we're due to take that bank . . . wot . . . two weeks . . . we can't afford complications, that woman isn't a loose cannon, she's a walking time bomb.'

'Maybe we should postpone.'

He put down his drink, laid a big hand on my shoulder, said, 'No can do old son, I need the cash.'

'What else is new.'

'Straight up . . . and you need to get that pistol back. Jaysus, all we need is for her to put a bullet in Bert.'

'Bert?'

'Yeah, the fast food guy, if she's as nutty as she sounds, she'll go back. It's what psychos do.'

Lisa, a barmaid, was collecting glasses. A friendly slip of a girl, I was always glad to see her. As she leant over, her breasts brushed my arm and she let the touch linger, her eyes locked on mine. Her perfume had a familiar scent . . . I asked, 'What's the fragrance?'

'Poison.'

'I don't doubt it but what's it called?'

'That's the name.'

It was what Cassie wore. Doc said, 'She fancies you, that Lisa does.'

'Leave it out.'

'C'mon, get the cork outa yer ass. Bring her home, have a nice uncomplicated lass for once.'

'Jeez, I haven't the energy.'

'Here, take this . . . it's amyl nitrate, crunch that baby under yer nose, you'll go like the clappers.'

'The fuck's going on. All day people feeding me poetry and dope or is that the other way round, dopes feeding me . . .'

'Poetry, dope and rock 'n' roll, like an Ian Dury song. Go on . . . go for it. Aren't I yer doctor.'

'You know I hate drugs.'

The sun through the bedroom window nudged me awake. I yawned, stretched, feeling *good*. Lisa woke and gave me a lazy smile. The door crashed open and Cassie was framed there, wearing one of my best shirts, screamed, 'Oh you bastard, how could you . . . in our marriage bed.'

Lisa's eyes were wide, she whispered, 'You're married!'

Cassie lunged forward, tore the sheet off, leaving us bare-assed.

'He didn't tell you . . . 'cos you're just another cheap whore . . . and young . . . the same age as our daughter.'

'Daughter!'

I moved and Cassie levelled the pistol. 'Do . . . and I'll shoot your balls off.'

The barrel of the gun swung towards Lisa, she began to whimper.

Cassie said, 'You stay away from my man, you hear me. You wanna suck on something, try this.'

And squeezed the trigger.

The bullet slammed into the headboard between us. Splinters of wood flying outwards. Lisa curled up in a ball, screaming. Now Cassie turned to me, asked, 'Did you memorise the lines?'

'What?'

'Tut-tut . . . it's the dunce's cap for you, hot shot. Alas, I must bid adieu. What's that shit you guys say here . . . tootle-pip . . . cheery-bye, whatever . . . later dude.'

She backed out and closed the door. I tried to put my arm round Lisa but she slapped it away, her crying got louder and full-blown hysteria got set. I pulled her round, slapped her face, measuring out the words.

'Shut the fuck up.'

She did.

I threw on a pair of jeans and a sweatshirt, headed cautiously to the front room. On the coffee table, in a glass, was one fresh red rose. I sighed . . . 'cute'. Made some scalding hot tea, laced it with sugar. The best remedy for shock, my hands were doing an Oirish jig . . . no, downright hornpipes. So, I got the brandy, poured some dollops in. As I held the bottle I thought . . . fuck . . . and took a swig. Hell to Henry, it burned like a sucker punch to the gut.

Took the tea to Lisa who was sobbing quietly. Forced the mug into her two hands.

She said, 'Don't want it.'

'Drink the fuckin' thing.'

'You bastard, never said you were married.'

'I'm not. She must have found the spare keys when she was here yesterday.'

And argh . . . could have bitten my tongue for adding yesterday. The fuck was wrong with me, I was a mine of information, mister extra detail.

'Yesterday . . . you had her here YESTERDAY and then brought ME here last night?'

Before she could get into full shout, I snapped her off.

'Leave it alone . . . OK . . . just drink the bloody tea.'

She took a sip, said, 'It's too sweet, don't you have Sweetex.'

'Hey . . . hey Lisa, cut me a bit o' slack . . . alright?'

'Are you going to call the Old Bill?'

'No, I'm going to call the doctor.'

'Don't need the doctor.'

'I sure as hell do.'

He came round in twenty minutes. Today he was wearing a bright green tracksuit that had the logo 'Charlton's Arms', and white Doc Martens. I'd never seen them in white, asked, 'I thought you only ever wore black ones.'

'So . . . I can't change. Is this what you called me for, to talk footwear?'

Lisa was in the shower, I was in tatters and told him the events. He gave a slow whistle.

'A raven.'

'What?'

'Lunatic . . . she's completely ape-shit.'

'That's your diagnosis, lucky I called you, else I wouldn't have known.'

'Yo Cooper, none of your lip, I didn't shoot at you but you're not too big for a flaming good puck in the mouth.'

Doc picked up a piece of paper, scanned it, said, 'Think this is for you, fella.'

I guess it was meant to accompany the rose, it read:

> 'Gotta keep it together
> while I'm falling apart'
>
> (Martina McBride)

I didn't know who the fuck this was, asked, 'Who the fuck's this?'

Doc laughed, said, 'A country and western singer and if I may say so *me fein*, a real cutie pie.'

I balled it, flicked it across the room, said, 'Jeez, the whole thing's like a bad country and western song.'

'I did some reading on your account last night.'

'On my account.'

'Yeah, checked out MacNeice, best if you know who you're dealing with.'

'And?'

'That's right Coop, be grateful, it's probably what you do best.'

'You're going to tell me or wot, you want what . . . flattery . . .?'

'Yeah, you're so good at it. OK, here goes. He was born in 1907 in Belfast. His oul lad was a Church of Ireland clergyman and you know what happens to their offspring.'

'What?'

''Ary Jaysus, don't you read the *News of The World*?

What class of ignoramus are you. Anyway, he's regarded as the poor fourth.'

'How do you mean?'

'In relation to the big three . . . C.S. Lewis, Auden, and Stephen Spender. No doubt you're familiar with those boyos.'

'Sure.'

'I thought so. He had a brother with Down's Syndrome.'

'So?'

'So Orson Welles had a brother who was mentally handicapped and his father had him locked away for ten years after which he became a social worker. A natural progression you might say. David Bowie has a brother who was also hidden away.'

I threw up my arms, said, 'Enough, you've gone a tad too Irish for me.'

Doc gave a hard stare at his footwear, said, 'Any chance of a sup of tea, here I am trying to wise you up, you won't as much as wet a man's whistle.'

Lisa came out of the bedroom wearing one of my shirts. At this rate I'd be shirtless. I already was clueless. I didn't mention it, just old-fashioned gallantry I guess. But Doc leapt in.

'I recognise the shirt but the coleen, now surely 'tis not the bould Lisa, you filthy article, what would your mother say?'

Lisa didn't blush but her body language tried to convey she knew the feeling, answered, 'My mum would say, I hope you took precautions.'

I was with her mother, she sure got my vote. Doc said, 'Do you like me shoes.'

'They're white!'

'Aye, as pure as the driven, any chance you'd give a man a drop of tea?'

She did. I had another jolt of coffee. I wasn't in the

mood for pissing about with tea, I wanted my caffeine naked and lethal. Doc asked her, 'You wouldn't know what a spike is me girl?'

'Like on a railing?'

'No, like a shelter for homeless men. Years ago when the drink had a grip, I went down the shitter and ended up in Gordon Road. Not just once either. Well, if you'd been living rough, they de-loused you.'

He paused to sip the tea and Lisa said, 'How awful.'

''Twas that and all. Then they gave you a white boiler suit. God in heaven, the mortification! You stood shivering in them white suits and everyone knew you'd been sprayed.'

'Was it dangerous?'

'Compared to what? You tied yer shoes round yer neck while you slept, if such a thing could be had among a multitude of farting roaring men. But the smell . . . ah . . . now there's a memory.'

'Of urine . . . and . . . things?'

'That . . . sure, but I meant the other. The very smell of desperation, of lost men in a lost place.'

I'd heard this yarn before so figured I'd shower. It's not a story you like better through repetition. As I shaved, I could hear his soft brogue.

'There was a fella there . . . Grogan. He gave viciousness a bad name, he'd steal the eye outa yer head and blame you. Men hold on to any shred of individuality . . . anything to mark you from the horde. His trademark was his boots, the old Doc Martens. One night in February, a cold bastard of a Friday, I heard him thrashing. Nothing unusual in that but I looked up anyway and saw two fellas moving away from his bunk.'

Lisa gave an excited cry.

'They were stealing his shoes?'

'They'd tried but the bastard had sea-manned the laces, merchant navy knots, and they'd strangled him.'

'Oh my God!'

'Yeah . . . but I got them loose.'

'You saved his life.'

'No, I saved his boots.'

Lisa left shortly after and the Doc said, 'You could do worse, in fact you've frequently done worse.'

'Thanks. So what do you reckon on this Cassie lunatic?'

'I'll put the word out, how hard can she be to find. Plus, I think she'll stay close, she seems fond of you.'

'You don't think I need get another shooter.'

'Naw, I'll do it, a fella offered me a grand yoke last week, I was going to buy it anyway.'

'What is it?'

'A Smith and Wesson 38. The Bodyguard Airweight one. It holds a little heavy in yer hand but I like that.'

'Where'd he get it?'

'You know those holiday apartments over in Kensington, the Arabs rent them? Turning one of those over, he found it in the fridge.'

'On ice so to speak.'

'Yeah. Best of all, it has a shrouded hammer.'

'Which does what exactly?'

'Stops it tangling if you're carrying it in yer pocket.'

'Ammunition?'

'Does the Pope have beads.'

The first bank we took was in Chingford. Yeah, like that, how many folks have you met who've been there . . . let alone heard of it. These small areas, who'd rob them . . . who'd bother. Yet they usually hold a shitpile of money. Can't be bothered moving it on and security is a joke. We didn't see it as a career move, we were hurting for readies and didn't want to play in our own manor. Doc said to me, 'I'd like to rob a bank in Chingford.'

'They have a bank?'

'Let's find out.'

First we had to find the whorin' place. But even then, the pattern was being set. We 'borrowed' a car in Ealing and hit off. Went in hard. Wearing balaclavas and boiler suits, shouting like fuck. I thought all the roaring was to intimidate the customers and staff. But it's to keep you rolling, keep you hyper. It was so easy, they near threw the money at us. In and out in six minutes and the buzz was so manic, we took down the post office as well. Fuck knows, we'd have gone in the building society but they'd closed. I was cooking, a white energy moving through me, like sex, I wanted to rob every premises on the High Street. Doc grabbed my arm, shouted, 'Enough, let's go . . . get a fucking grip on yourself.'

Burned rubber outa there and tore off the masks. Those fuckin' things are hot and itchy. As I hit fourth gear, revving like a lunatic, I glanced at Doc. He felt it too. Rivers of sweat pouring down his face and his eyes like major bullets, near popping out of his skull. The back seat was jammed with money. We knew we'd been incredibly lucky and blatantly stupid. But the foundation was good and I could see a blueprint for serious profit.

It was intended as a one-off, for walking round money. That evening, at Doc's flat, he said, 'You really got off on that, yeah.'

'Fuckit, I never expected to take so much. If we're not careful, we might be bordering on actual fuckin' wealth here.'

'That's not what I meant.'

'You're not happy with the cash, take less, what's the matter with you.'

'You liked it . . . the job I mean . . . no . . . you adored it. I've never seen you so . . . gimme a word . . .'

'Delighted?'

'Animated . . . electrified . . . you were all lit up.'

'Still am.'

'You've found the thing that everybody wants.'

'Wot's that then, mega bucks?'

'Don't be an eejit Cooper. Something that brings them out of the herd, lets them kiss the heavens and fly, to soar on high.'

'Doc . . . hey . . . lighten up . . . OK. We're loaded, we robbed a bank . . . we're not banged up . . . it's not bloody religion.'

'But that's exactly it, you found religion, you'll be doing this again . . . and again.'

We'd bought half a dozen bottles of Johnny Walker, three dozen cans of special and a shit heap of Chinese. I took the whisky straight from the bottle, let it coast and burn, popped some chow mein and washed it down with beer. Let the whole shebang blend, pour the friggin' works, let them go figure what sent where, I asked, 'Saying you're right, let's just suppose you are, where does that leave you?'

He didn't answer for a bit, then, 'With you . . . wot else, you mad bastard. How does Huntingdon sound, like the ring?'

I did . . . Staines, Milton Keynes, Crawley, Kidderminster, Haysham, East Trilling, . . . away days . . . and the mountain of cash began to shape. But, you've got to have a front. The old Bill are going to come sniffin' sure as shooting. You need chameleon image. What you can show but can't be pinned down. They look you over, yer business could be gold, could be shite.

Repo men. Yeah . . . that's what we put out. Ain't it the way of the world though, how it turns. First you got to get it, then you've got to bloody hide it. 'GOD REPOSSESSES AND SO DO WE'.

It wasn't going to hurt me to be up to me ass in cars. Money follows money. We rented a lock-up in Victoria, got the phone in and put small ads in the trades, in the locals. Here's what it read:

'Cat got yer tongue
they've got yer car
if you want to re-possess
give us a bell
THE R.R. (RIGHTEOUS REPO).'

And fuck me, ain't it rich, the business took off. According to the Met, there's a car nicked every two seconds in inner London alone. Jeez we were swamped. Had to take on staff and rent more space. Exciting too, see how long it took to track and move a vehicle. Then the movie came out, *Repo Man* with Emilio Estevez. Business boomed. I half fancied I was a touch like Emilio meself, that broody dark shit . . . yeah. You figure we packed in the banks? Never happen, no way. The Doc had my number. It was my very adrenaline, the juice in my veins. Sure, I liked the repo, the cars it brought me in contact with, the money, but it was like comparing a hand job to wild sex, a spoon of shandy up against a bottle of Walker.

We figured on a few rules early. No partners, strictly a two-man operation. If it needed more, then pack it in. Trust no one. The Doc had a prayer for us:

'God keep us smart, fast
and mobile
the rest we'll handle
ourselves.'

Seems God was listening. Then.

We must have got Him on a good day. Thing is, I reckon He enjoys a bit of villainy too. Else how to account for the Tory party. And mostly what we got was careful. Kevin Costner as Elliot Ness in *The Untouchables* is urged by his wife to be careful. He says, 'like mice at a crossroads'.

Learnt the shit as we went along too. Out with the wool balaclavas, got us some light cotton jobs. No cumbersome gloves either. Those surgical skin-fit ones that make people instinctively edgy.

Experimented with the art of deception. The Doc would wear a larger size shoe and we're talking big here, and bring along flour or baking soda. Sprinkle some of that on our way in and leave a nice clear print. Jeez, the filth adore a cosy fat clue. I had some fun with tattoos, those washable chaps. Put 'I Love Me Old Mum' in bold letters on my arm and let the sleeve ride up as I scooped the cash. Some whiz-kid bank trainee was hot to trot. A major breakthru for the investigation. After that one, half the old lags who lived with their Mums were rounded up. Even the Krays got a shout. Accents too, throw in some rasta and half of Brixton got turned over. We didn't fuck with the Irish though. Doc said, 'The last . . . the very last thing we want . . . is for the boyos to get pissed with us.'

I took his word on that.

Neither of us smoked so we ensured we dropped butts on our exit and all over the abandoned motor. One raid, Doc procured insulin and left the half-empty phial under the seat. That made it to CrimeStoppers. Kept our mouths tight shut. No braggin', no hints, nada.

Things got hairy too. An old dear had a heart attack on our Hatton Cross job. Doc wanted to send flowers and cash. I lost it.

'The fuck you saying . . .? You want to be Robin Hood, is that it . . . have the public love us. Jeez, mebbe we could cut a record. We're in this for cash, not friggin' sentiment.'

He sent the cash anyway. I could have sent the flowers.

Arnold L. White. Is that a name or wot. Our accountant. I wasn't going to prison for VAT or any of that sneaky crap. He had an office in Camberwell. I had to ask, 'What's the L for?'

'Leopold.'

'You're winding me up.'

'Do I look like a kidder, as if humour is my forte?'

He didn't.

Looked like a sour priest and hey, that's how it should be. Money is a sacred business. He had a cheeky secretary named Iris, a pushy blonde, all mouth and nastiness.

I gave her one. Call it duty, to keep tabs on Leopold. She was the worst kind of leg-over . . . loud, came roaring and shouting as if I'd murdered her. The French call orgasm the little death. Guess they hadn't heard of Iris. No doubts with that lady, she knew what she wanted and rode the daylights outa me. After, she'd say, 'I'd kill for a bacon butty.'

She'd had a husband, Patrick, from County Kerry who'd gone MIA. The worst criminal ever to come outa Camberwell. Not dangerous, just useless. He'd attempted to rob a Pakistani shopkeeper, using a replica. The man near split his skull in two with a brick . . . a real one. Patrick got ten years. Prior to that, he'd been in a pub one night. A fella named Mick had given him a ferocious hiding. All Patrick remembered was the name. So, he packed a meat cleaver in an Adidas holdall and returned to the pub.

No sooner had he ordered, when the barman roared to a customer heading for the loo, 'How's about ye Mick.'

Patrick followed, missed with the cleaver, it was embedded in the wall. Mick and five of his mates then attempted to fit the cleaver to Patrick's arse-hole. After she'd told me this, she added drily, 'I said to 'im, you pathetic wanker, you like sex and travel so fuck off outa here.'

What Arnold also provided was information. Of the banking variety. Doc had a chat with him, suggested it would be mutual if the skinny on obscure banks were available. Their days for 'holding'.

Arnold was yer classic accountant. He asked no questions but one, a highly indignant tone, 'You think I can be bought?'

Doc named a figure.

He was bought.

Networking. Wot a lovely word:

Hip

Contemporary

Sassy.

Arnold networked a series of clerks in the major banks. Not too many, but sufficient to provide the dates without arousing suspicion.

It had risk . . . sure. The old fall-out factor, but it worked. Plus too, a clerk blew the whistle he was on the bank 'suss list'. Banks don't rate loyalty, only profit.

I'd put a portion of map on the wall, let the Doc have a look.

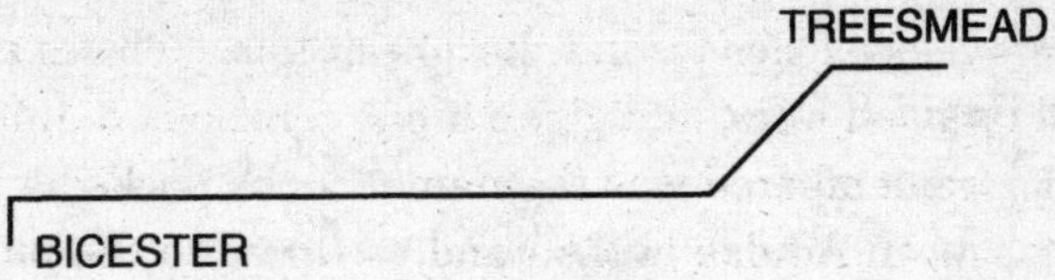

Asked, 'See anything you like?'

'Never heard of that Bicester, means we'd pass thru Morse country.'

'Put the wind up Sergeant Lewis, eh.'

Thursdays were best as the payrolls would be in but we didn't want to establish a pattern. Sooner or later though, you had to figure on getting a tug. I'd only recently moved to Meadow Road, was burning money with the decorators. Jeez, what is it with those fucks, all that shouting. I'd said, 'Hey . . . this isn't the Grand Canyon, you don't have to check for echo. Let's keep the damn shouting to a minimum. How would this be . . . if a roar has to be made, and I don't dispute the necessity, I'll do it . . . OK. I'm paying, so I'll be roaring.'

Which I think put it across rather well. An informed and civilised outlay of the rules. They listened almost attentively and then continued roaring.

'Hey Joe, where's my hammer? . . . Cyril, wot's gonna win the 3.30? . . . That Dettori ain't worth shit . . . Three sugars and a sausage sarnie . . .'

Yeah, like that. I was contemplating a short stay in a hotel but I liked to keep an eye on the fucks. The doorbell rang. Would one of the decorators answer? Course not . . .

'Not in my portfolio mate.'

I flung the door open, the hammerin' behind me a decibel louder. Two men in raincoats, the hard-eyed look.

You knew when they weren't flogging double glazing or Mormons. Coats were too cheap.

'Mr Cooper.'

'Yes.'

'Mr David Cooper.'

'Yes.'

'Sorry to trouble you Sir, I'm Chief Inspector Noble and this is Detective Sergeant Quinn, might we have a word?'

'Not a quiet one I'm afraid.'

'I beg your pardon?'

I gestured behind me. Noble gave a tight smile, humour not even distantly touching it. In his fifties, he'd the recent health of an ex-drinker and the tension it bestowed. I looked at my watch, said, 'Down the road, there's The Roebuck . . . very quiet at this hour, would that do . . . are ye allowed . . . fraternise in . . . public houses.'

A look passed between them said . . . 'got a friggin' live one.'

Quinn was thin, in his thirties. He'd the face of a greyhound gone rogue, a rabid light in his eyes. This guy liked to sink his teeth and never let up. The worst kind of cop, it was always personal with him. Noble said, 'In the line of duty, we could force ourselves I think.'

'Okey-dokey then, you lads scuttle on down there, I'll get my coat and be with you . . . in say . . . five, how would that be.'

'That would be fine, five minutes.'

I went and got my leather jacket, a Georgio Armani and it knows it. Leather so soft it croons, goes out by itself. I swear it wept when Brazil stole the World Cup. I'd met women who wanted an evening with the jacket. Makes me feel good and I needed that. Had figured they'd come but now, I didn't know was I ready. My body said. 'No you're not' and sweat made lakes on my torso. Ever have one of those situations, like the following. You're moving along the footpath, see a person coming towards you. In this instance, a woman in her late twenties, bit of a looker. Not earth shattering but cookin'. There's only the two of you, not another punter on the path. Bags of time to move easily by. Yet . . . and here's the fuck of it. Ye begin the manoeuvres early so as not to collide. Despite all the rules of gravity, you end up nose on nose, flappin' uselessly as ye attempt to get by. I smiled, one of those knowing world-weary jobs to say, 'Oh . . . silly us.' She gave a loud sigh of aggressive annoyance, said, 'Oh get out of my way for heaven's sake.'

I grabbed her arm, hissed, 'Hey, don't pissin' sigh at me lady, I'll break yer bloody face . . . hear me.'

Didn't affect her, as she moved on she shouted, 'Damn Yuppie.'

I guess it was the jacket.

I arrived in The Roebuck, up for it. The two were sitting at a corner table, untouched glasses of orange like prayers before them. I opened: 'On the old Britvics eh.'

'But let us not curtail . . . your inclinations.'

This from Noble, again the dead smile. I sat opposite them. The barman shouted, 'What'll it be guv?'

'Same as these chappies.'

He brought it over and it sat with the other immobile glasses. I said, 'Ah, the juice.'

Noble gave me the long look, said, 'Nice bit o' leather, expensive was it.'

'Are you in the market for one, that it?'

'Alas, a policeman's salary wouldn't run to such an item.'

The juice looked forlorn, I extended a finger, said, 'Eeny, Meeny, Miny . . . Mo.'

And Quinn spoke, South-East London hard, but inroads of Irish, 'Catch a blagger by the toe.'

Noble added, 'Quinn here is a plastic Paddy . . . second generation, he hates blaggers.'

'And who would blame him?'

'Precisely David. It is David isn't it . . . You don't mind if I call you that, or are you more comfortable with Davy or Dave even?'

'Cooper is fine.'

'Touch hard is it not, are you a hard man Dave?'

'Not according to my old mum, bless her heart.'

Quinn leaned over, 'You've got form Davy boy.'

'That's right.'

'And keeping clean, are yah?'

'With the decorating, it's not easy.'

His dog face was working up to it.

'Not hurting for the readies . . . business good, was it?'

I knew I could go either way. Kiss ass and have him enjoy it or, 'Ever keep greyhounds Quinn?'

'That's sergeant to you. Wotcha mean?'

'Oh nothing, you remind me of White City, I thought perhaps yer Dad was into them, know wot I mean?'

Noble cut in, but first a glance at Quinn that said 'Jeez, he *does* look like one!'

'Davy, we have a problem, there's been a string of bank jobs, all over the bloody shop. Two-man outfit, very pro, very classy. Would you know anything about these?'

'Can't help you there, repo is what I do.'

Noble sighed.

'I feel it in my water Dave that you could help us, wouldn't do for the nick to repossess you.'

The barman came over, asked, 'Is the orange off or wot?'

Quinn didn't look up, said, 'Fuck off.'

He did.

Noble stood and gestured to Quinn, who kept his eyes locked on me, said, 'We'll be in touch Dave, I just know you're going to be a big help.'

When they were gone, I carried the glasses over to the bar, said, 'Sorry about those wankers, mebbe you could recycle these.'

He slung 'em down the sink, said, 'Naw, they're friggin' contaminated, am I right.'

'Absolutely.'

Three days passed, no sign or light of Cassie. Doc had the heavy word out but no show. I began to relax, figured she'd headed for higher ground. Kept thinking of her though, the leather sex, the bloody chemistry of the crazy bitch. But I knew I was better off without her. The hell of it is, trouble is so exciting and I'd been sliding along, not bored but heart not beating rapid either. The repo business was doing good and I'd gone to Brixton to suss out a major job. Done that and drifted into the big pub on the corner. Ordered mash and a banger, half a bitter. Found a table at the window and dug in. Never heard her till she sat opposite, she glanced at the food, said, 'No shit Cooper, but is that phallic or wot.'

I cut the sausage, hefted a wedge and she licked her bottom lip, whispered, 'Give it to me big boy.'

'Fuck off.'

'You want me to haul ass.'

'Yeah . . . and give me back the bloody gun.'

'Aw-righty,' she said, and opened her bag.

'Jeez, not here, what . . . are you outa yer tree.'

'Well outa federal jurisdiction. I wanna make up.'

'Make up, like stories is it?'

'I'm hot for you Cooper. I could service you now, under the table. You just go on eating your vitals, all your appetites satisfied together.'

'Go away.'

She touched her hair, asked, 'Do I look like Jennifer Aniston?'

'Who?'

'Oh Gawd. Don't you watch TV . . . like, you never heard of *Friends*?'

'I've got the Doc.'

'JES-US . . . like get real. It's a comedy series, like mega. A million women copied Jennifer's style. There's even a cult called "The Holy Tabernacle of Aniston The Divine".'

'Don't mean shit to me but yer hair . . . is . . . I dunno . . . circa Cathy McGowan . . . the 60s . . . like that.'

She rolled her eyes and that closed the hair rap. Said, 'I bought you a present.'

'Keep it.'

'Please Cooper just let me explain. I was jealous, it makes me crazy, I never met a man like you. Mind if I smoke.'

'And you'll refrain if I do.'

She took out the Camels, soft pack and crushed, shook one free, asked, 'Can you light me?'

A couple in their twenties, laden with food, approached and asked, 'Might we share your table?'

Cassie's head turned, spat, 'What, you goddamn blind, we look like we're receiving company? Can't you see we're having sex here.'

I jumped up, said, 'Sure, we're all finished.'

And strode out. She was right on my heels as I hit the path, shouted, 'Don't leave me, what about the children.'

You can do just about any weird shit in Brixton and no one gives a toss. Ain't nothing new. But she got attention, maybe it was the bloody Yank accent. A group of the brothers were hanging outside the blues music shop, one of them said, 'No way to treat a lady, man.'

I said, without breaking my stride, 'That's no lady, it's the shoplifter from hell.'

As I moved fast into Coldharbour Lane, her voice carried: 'I love you David and Louis MacNeice.'

I dunno if it meant Louis loved me too but I doubt it. Got the car keys out and my hands were shaking. Half expected her to start shooting. The engine revved and I burned rubber, sweat dancing on my upper lip.

Back home I got right on the phone, called a mate, asked, 'You still fitting locks?'

'Sure.'

'OK, can you do a rush job, like now?'

'Naw, we're booked solid, no can do old son.'

'If I throw in a few ponies for yourself.'

'What time would suit you?'

'And shoot the works OK, deadbolts, state-of-the-art shit, top of the line.'

'It will cost.'

'Tell me about it. What's the best system?'

'The three five seven.'

'What?'

'Magnum.'

'Get here soonest, leave the humour at the office.'

Poured a Scotch, took a fast slug, muttered 'crazy bloody bitch' and rang Doc.

'That you Coop, how's she cutting?'

'I found her.'

'Good man, where?'

'Brixton.'

'Figures. Did you deal with her?'

'We had lunch.'

'What? Are you stone raving mad. Tell me at least you got the shooter back, tell me that.'

'I managed to get away from her.'

'I'm confused Cooper, or you're winding me up. We've been hunting her, half the firm on overtime, me calling in favours from every breed of wanker and you're saying *you* escaped.'

'I'm going to change the locks.'

'Fuck-me-pink, you need to change your bloody attitude.'

He hung up.

A large package arrived next morning. The postman had to ring as it took me ages to undo the new locks. Grunting, I pulled open the door. As he handed me the package he winked. I asked, 'Something wrong with yer eye mate?'

'Nothing wrong with ME.'

'Keep that up, it will change.'

And slammed the door. Scrawled all over the paper was 'S.W.A.L.K., a heart, I love you stallion, and LIPS'. I said, jeez, who could this be? Tore it open, praying to hell-and-gone it wasn't incendiary. I already knew it was explosive, a book fell out. *Autumn Journal* by Louis MacNeice. Swore, this fuck again. I was very tired of the guy. Still, the book had a nice feel to it. Old leather cover, gold-leaf pages and one of them index fingies you see in bibles. She'd written a note, what a surprise.

'My David, David Mia
Without you
What warehouse of the soul
awaits me now.'

Deep, I said, very friggin' deep.

I used the index and read:

'And I remember Spain
at Easter, ripe as an egg
for revolt and ruin
though for a tripper
the rain was worse
than the surly
or the worried or the haunted faces.'

I wasn't getting this. Maybe he was one of those guys you had to hear aloud. So I cleared my throat, looked around a bit self-consciously and took my shot.

'The churches full of saints
tortured on racks of marble
and the Escorial
cold for ever

within the heart of Philip
as if veneer could hold
the rotten guts
and crumpled bones together.'

Yeah, well, some people had a flair for it. The Doc, now he'd read the telephone directory and you felt moved. I reckon the Irish always sound as if they mean it, as if it's personal. Us lot, we've always one ear open for the hint of ridicule.

My old man, he fancied his voice. Sunday evenings he'd read to my mother and I from the Good Book. All the Old Testament stuff. Jeez, he was hot for that fire and brimstone, unmerciful punishments and ferocious suffering. The torment of the damned got him hot. Silly fucker would drone on about begots and begats. My mother punctuating the silences with compliments and praise, she can't have been right in the head, or could she possibly have been taking the piss? How I wish it were so. Truth is, she was the worst kind of criminal. She supported him in his tyranny of bullying and beatings, encouraged him in the nurture of those fuckin' pigeons. The face of gentility and aspiring middle class, she was the public face of the beast. After he took his dive, she became a professional widow, leapt into black weeds and wore them like a trophy. 'Hey – see me – not only had I a husband but I buried him *and* of course, there'll be no other man.' As if anyone would have the cow. I got the fuck away from her as soon as I was able and it wasn't soon enough.

Long before the psychologists, the heart-juicers came trippin' along with fancy names like dysfunctional, our family unit was full fledged fucked.

The old man's Christian name was Alistair. Not that he'd a drop of Christianity. He had a framed tapestry in our pokey hall which said:

MAN PROPOSES
GOD DISPOSES

Yeah.

Alistair the righteous, the unholy more like. Don't think he'd planned on bein' 'smote' from a three-storey building in Battersea, not a howl down from the dogs' home. One might say he was indeed begot, or is it begat. Whatever, well creamed any road. The doorbell went. I didn't recognise him at first, then he spoke.

'Dave, how are you lad, have you forgotten me?'

Then it clicked. Noble, the noble savage.

'Chief Inspector.'

'One and the same, I must put my hand up, cop a plea. That's police manual humour to put Joe Public at ease.'

'It works, or is it to put him off his guard?'

'Might I step in?'

'Have you a warrant?'

Took him aback. I added, 'Just kiddin', come on then.'

He had a cheap raincoat and even cheaper aftershave. No, the cheapest. It comes free with the litre bottles of bleach.

'Have a seat.'

As he did he took a full look round.

'The decorators did you proud, very nice job, local lads are they?'

'By means of Dublin.'

'Expensive?'

'Depends on your perspective Inspector. Tea, coffee, vodka. No, hold the phones, I've a nice bit o' Britvic.'

He smiled, said, 'Perhaps the tea.'

I got that done, put cups, milk, sugar on a tray and some strawberry jam delights. Put the spread before him, he said, 'Now, isn't this cosy.'

And took a biscuit, bit cautiously, said, 'Mm . . . m . . . that is good, Marks and Spencers?'

'Sainsbury's.'

'First class. I might go another.'

And he did. Then said, 'Bit o' news you'll find fascinating.'

'Oh yeah, and what would that be?'

'The Met are to be issued with longer acrylic batons. The Home Secretary wanted to know if the longer length made a difference in physical impact injuries and has finally approved them.'

'That is fascinating. Acrylic eh, and machine washable.'

'I doubt you'd pop them in yer local laundrette. Meanwhile, the villains load up on Uzis and M-11's.'

'I do appreciate your hoppin' round to tell me, Inspector but you could have phoned.'

'And miss these treats, I do believe I'll have another. That your Astra outside?'

'It's a repo, I'll drop it off later.'

'Don't doubt it for a minute. Who's going to play silly buggers eh? The reason I wished to see you is, I wondered if you'd any new ideas on those robberies.'

'Not a one.'

'Mm . . . m . . . you're not having tea.'

'Bit early for me.'

'We know it's the same two men. They nick a car and hit at random, almost like they stuck a pin in a map. What do you think?'

'No idea.'

'Well, that's my job eh, but I'll pop round from time to time let you know how the investigation's going.'

He stood up, noisily drained his cup, headed for the door. I said, 'It isn't really necessary you know.'

'Of course I know it isn't fuckin' necessary Cooper. When it gets to that, I'll send Quinn.'

Doc was close to shouting.

'What did you do to antagonise the prick.'

'Do me a bloody favour Doc, I gave him tea for crying out loud.'

'And he definitely said WHEN not IF.'

'You think I misheard him, that it?'

'Fuck fuck fuck.'

'That's a big help.'

I was round at Doc's place. He lived off the Clapham Road in an old draughty house that never got warm. Laura, his common-law wife, was doing household shit and noisily. A small intense brunette, she'd a vicious temper. I don't think she liked me but it wasn't personal. She didn't like anybody, even Doc seemed to bug her and they'd been together eighteen years. He shouted, 'Laura, for fuck's sake, will you stop bangin' things.'

'When you stop bangin' young wans.'

He gave a huge smile, said, 'The mouth on that woman, strip paint off a gate. Hey Laura, wet a sup o' tea.'

'Wet it yerself.'

They had a sixteen-year-old daughter, currently at a posh boarding school. Doc said, 'Everyone in this household does time.'

Laura sighed, 'But I'm the only one doing life.'

Round at Lisa's, I'd called with flowers. The logo shouts

'Say It With Flowers'. A bunch of pink roses, they didn't have a whole lot of chat. Lisa said, 'They're lovely.'

What else could she add. She'd answered the door in nowt but a slip.

'How does the postman react?' I asked.

'To what.'

Well fuckit, cancel the witty repartee. She gave me a large scotch and as I got behind that, I noticed she'd a gold chain round her ankle.

'Why do you wear a chain on yer foot?'

'It's called a slave bracelet.'

'That must set women's rights back a few years.'

Not appreciated. Anger made her face ugly, blended with the knowledge she'd suspected the very same thing.

'Are you calling me a bimbo?'

'Whoa, slow down babe, you can hang it from your ass, see if I could give a fuck.'

She bent down to get a book, giving me a flash that hit like hope.

'I read things you know. Look, I've got Carrie Fisher's book.'

'One of the greats.'

'Do you read her?'

'Bloody hell, I can almost quote her.'

'Do you know this bit?

"Here's how men think:
Sex
Work
Food
Sports
Relationships." '

She looked so eager as she read this. I felt a complete

bastard but I'd signed on, so I said, 'Not much escapes the bold Carrie. And, how do women score.'

'Oh she's so right, she says women think:

"Relationships
Relationships
Relationships
Work
Sex
Shopping
Weight
Food." '

I said, 'Wanna sit over here babe?'

'OK.'

I got my hand under that slip and got hot. As we got to the deposit till, she pushed me off, said, 'Don't be so rough.'

Alas, I'd gone a tad too far down the jackpot road, was in the area of sexual bravado, whispered, 'You're a slave, do what the master commands.'

And she threw a drink in my face. I roared, 'The fuck you think you're doing?'

'I want to be wooed.'

'What!'

'Romance – and the cinema. You don't respect me.'

I stood up, headed out, added quiet, 'Bolix.' I wanted only Cassie, blind to all else.

The flowers were by the door but they'd nowt to add, not even goodbye.

Outside, I experienced the sense of being stalked. I had to figure it could be cops but it was too eerie. Physically shook myself to get back on track. Muttered 'get real', or failing that, 'get real bloody vicious'.

I'd been handling Cassie all wrong. Coming on hardass

was where she lived. If there was a next time, I'd be Mr Diplo-fuckin'-matic till I cornered. Then, we'd rock 'n' roll.

A wino was witnessing 'I was never a social drinker, only a social security drinker.' I'd asked Doc if his boozin' had been as serious as he told it. He'd answered, 'Lemme put it this way. I was living in Bradford for six months before I realized it was Darlington.'

Quite.

I still had the Astra, I dunno why. It's a woman's car in truth. If you need a second car, then it's as good as any. But for the main event, the numero uno, the big friggin' cheese, it's window dressing. Got home and planned a slow evening of strong drink. The phone went.

'Dave?'

'Yeah . . . hey . . . Doc, is that you?'

He never called me by my Christian name, I actively discouraged it. Only when heavy shit went down did he resort to it. Right now, I'd swear he was sobbing, his voice sounded broken.

'Dave, it's Laura – she's dead.'

'What!'

'It's true Dave – she went under a train . . . oh God.'

Now he was sobbing, I said, 'I'm on my way buddy, just hang tight . . . OK.'

'OK.'

The flaming Astra wouldn't start. Then I realized I was flooding the engine and forced myself to calm down . . . OK . . . OK . . . try again. Burned rubber outa there.

As I drove I could hear Doc in my head, the thousand things he'd said. Once, 'You never hear of Tom Leonard?'

'No.'

'Ah, you ignoramus, he proposed that long-term prisoners be given the freedom to purchase their own cells.'

The police cars were parked outside his house. I went in and came face to face with Quinn. What appeared dangerously close to a smirk was plastered on his greyhound snout. He nodded.

Doc was sitting in an armchair, a bottle of Scotch between his legs. I crouched down, said, 'I'm so sorry buddy.'

He looked blank, asked, 'I dunno, should I drink whisky, Laura says it makes me cranky.'

'How about some tea?'

'I'd like some tea, two sugars please.'

A uniformed cop was in the kitchen, his shoulder microphone emitting squawky messages. I asked, 'Do you know what happened?'

'It seems she'd been shopping and was changing trains at the Oval for the Northern Line to Morden. She went under at approximately five forty-five. Rush hour, it didn't half bugger up the timetable. We got her name from her handbag.'

I made the tea, the cop's mike was eating at my nerves, I snapped, 'Can't you shut that bloody thing off.'

'No can do Sir, any chance of a cuppa?'

I gave him the look, said, 'No can do pal, know wot I mean?'

Doc took the tea but was unsure what to do. I said, 'Drink it.'

'OK.'

He took his reading glasses from the table before him. I thought 'Wot, he's going to read *now*,' and he said, 'Can I have a glass of water?'

Before I could act, he began to feverishly polish the lens, saying 'This was not a boating accident.'

For that moment, he was Richard Dreyfuss in *Jaws* and then he switched channels. This is a case for the 87 Precinct, Steve Carella and Bert Kling. Meyer Meyer was as bald as an egg – 'let's hear it for the deaf man' – Steve's wife, Teddy, was a mute. Carver City and the boys of the eighty-seven. Shit, I nearly forgot Lieutenant Byrnes. I looked up and Quinn was there, said, 'Yer mate's losing it', the Doc's gone doolally.'

I said, 'Let's take this outside.'

Before I could get into it, he said, 'I hate to laugh and run but, it seems you'll need a new partner, it being a two-man job.'

'You want to explain that Quinn?'

'Yer repos – I mean wot else are you two into?'

I'd clenched my fists, never had I wanted to take down a guy so bad, I could taste blood in my mouth, said, 'You like to put it in people's faces Quinn, get right in there and fuck. Keep it up.'

He gave a huge grin, 'Oh, I intend to. Next time you have an away day, that you take a wee excursion, I'll be there. You're all mine Cooper.'

'Good, I'll be looking forward to it . . . you mangy piece of shit.'

Returning to Doc, I took it as a positive sign that he was drinking the tea. He said, 'According to Freud, a man doesn't become a man till his father dies, so I wonder what he reverts to when his partner goes.'

'From the evidence, a babbling idiot.'

He turned to look right into my face, added, 'She really didn't like you.'

Jeez, thanks a bunch Doc, I needed to hear this now. I didn't say anything. Gave one of them wise head-nodding gestures, reeking of understanding. But, he thought I wasn't getting it, grabbed my arm tightly, 'No, I'm serious Davey. She didn't care for most people, but she fuckin' loathed you.'

I tried to interpret this as grief but, if he kept it up, he'd really be in bloody shock. 'She said you were a cold fish, that beneath your frosty exterior was more ice.'

I thought she'd had a rough deal. Doc's years in prison, his uncertain future, her horrendous death . . . and then I thought . . . fuck her.

The funeral was huge, villains like the full show. Cops came too though not in a mourning capacity. What a display of cars! I once read Maurice Gibb describe success. Remember him, the Bee Gees. He said he was standing at his front door looking at a street packed with motors and knew, 'They're all mine.' I looked at the line of vehicles and knew, they're all repos.

Noble came, same lousy raincoat, said, 'She was a good 'un.'

'You knew her?'

'Never laid an eye on her – or a finger – but what the hell else is there to say.'

Doc looked downright elegant. Black suit, tie, and the manic-shined black Martens. His daughter, Emma, was out from the boarding school. A flash little piece of jail-bait, she asked me, 'Did you know my Mum?'

'She was a good 'un.'

'I don't think she liked you.'

Great.

The reception was Irish, booze and food. Doc was in the middle of the crowd, stories chasin' the whisky, or is that vice-versa. Anyway, like that. He was saying, 'So this wanker takes a look at me, sees I'm a big 'un, says I used to be scared of a couple of blokes . . . I says yeah . . . and I'm the both of 'em.'

Maybe it was the wedding he'd never had. I strolled over to read the condolences. A mountain of them, you'd swear Laura had a lock on Mother Theresa. The tributes to a woman who never was. I felt if no one had showed, Laura would have respected that. One card I had to pick up, it read:

With gravest respects,
Louis MacNeice

'What!'

Doc touched my arm, said, 'Can I get you a bit o' grub, a drink?'

'No . . . no thanks, you don't have to play host . . . OK.'

'Jaysus, don't bite the face off me, I'm just trying to be hospitable.'

'What? Oh right – look Doc, I'm sorry, it's just there's something weird going on.'

Doc pushed a drink into my hand, asked, 'Are we still on?'

'You mean next week. Jeez, I dunno – under the circumstances, shouldn't we, you know.'

'You think I'm not bloody up to it. Don't worry about me fella, I'll keep my end up.'

'No, I mean, the cops are all over us.'

'And, if we don't go it's as plain as a confession.'

'But better than actually getting caught.'

Doc swallowed a huge drink. Didn't knock a feather outa him, gave me the no shit stare, said, 'Dave, I have to have this money, OK . . .'

'We're not hurting.'

He slapped his forehead with the heel of his hand, said, 'Will yah listen to him! I'm up to me arse with school fees, the memorial to Laura . . .'

'The what?'

'In marble. I promised Father Cleary the new Church wing would be Laura's wish.'

I couldn't believe it, said, 'I can't believe it. We'll be in the wing – on friggin' Parkhurst.'

'Are you with me or not Dave.'

What could I do. He was the only person ever to fight my corner.

'OK . . . but.'

'Good man, now drink up – you'd think it was your funeral.'

I went back later to get the condolence card but it was gone. A bad feeling like talking death was all over me, whisperin' – 'soon'.

Father Cleary was early sixties – I'm not referring to his age. He had that aura of optimism and stupidity. You just knew he hummed the Beatles. Couple that with the air of the professional beggar and you'd a near-lethal cocktail. He approached me with gusto and I thought, 'Watch yer wallet.'

His greeting, 'Ah, Mr Collins I do declare.'

'It's Cooper.'

'Really?'

He sounded as if he'd never quite reconciled himself to liars, then, 'Are you sure. Ho ho, listen to me, course you're sure. I wanted to thank you for the generosity of your donation from the firm.'

'It's nothing.'

'Too modest Mr C. You're not of our persuasion, I take it, which makes it even more magnificent.'

'That's one word for it.'

'You're not an atheist I trust.'

'Presbyterian.'

'Same thing.'

'I beg your pardon?'

'Just joking, some ecclesiastical humour.'

'Is that what it is. My father was a God-fearing man.'

'And passed over has he – the poor creature.'

'Took off actually.'

He gave a look round, time up for me but I figured I'd hold him a bit as he gave his exit line.

'Laura had a grand send off.'

'I thought you guys, the R.C.'s, frowned on suicide.'

He prepared his smile, more of the e-humour: 'Naturally we don't encourage it but an air of leniency exists nowadays. For example, we don't insist on ceremony or titles so much. You needn't call me Father, you can call me Pat.'

'Why on earth would I wanna do that?'

And he hadn't a reply. His smile dissolved, so I gave him a playful push, a forceful one, added, 'Hey, lighten up Padre, that's a little repo humour. Isn't God after all, the ultimate repo man.'

And left him to it.

No doubt he could work it into a sermon. Very little got

by him save the invention of dry cleaning. He'd had the shiniest black pants I'd ever seen, from pure wear. Made of Terylene, remember that. The sheen accessorised the spit in his soul.

GUNS

As I left the funeral, I near said festivities and maybe that was more accurate. Doc grabbed my arm, 'You're leggin' it already.'

'Yeah, I'm funned out.'

'Oh, that's rich Cooper.'

'Was there something?'

'Hardware. We're gonna need some shooters right – the guy fell thru but I got another address. Here, you go arm us.'

'But this is in Islington.'

'What, you think they only sell guns in Kilburn?'

'Bad fuck to this – I dunno this guy.'

'He's expecting you.'

'Wonderful, thing is what's he expecting from me?'

'Cash, lotsa cash.'

'How novel.'

But Doc had already turned away. Father Cleary was calling. I wanted to go to Islington about as much as I'd want an evening with Quinn. Traffic was light and I got over there in jig time. The day's repo was the Renault Espace Turbo Diesel. A sort of double retake as the company was recalling them, to install a fuse in the engine's diesel pre-heating system. Heat sometimes damaged the wiring harness. What I did was be careful. Enough heat going down already. Couldn't find the house for ages. Saw a size nine and toyed with asking, 'Know where the gun dealer hangs his shingle?'

Then bingo! Got outa the door and locked it by remote

from the pavement. It gives that 'ping' so beloved by yuppies everywhere. Shit, all I needed was the cellular and I'd be the total asshole. Rang the doorbell – the door opened a crack.

'Yes.'

'Are you Joseph?'

'Who wants to know?'

'Look, I feel ridiculous saying this but Doc sent me. He forgot to give me a password, his secret service training ain't what it used to be.'

'Come in.'

Nice clean house, not a gun in sight. Nice clean gun dealer too. Joseph was in his mid-twenties, crew cut and Miami Vice casuals. Loose shirt, pants and, we hoped not loose-tongued. He had a corduroy face as if someone sat on it and it didn't bounce back. Dark eyes with fire. Doc hadn't mentioned the guy was a dance short on his card, light on the feet. Not yer screaming queen but it was there. He gave me the smile, puts lots of teeth in it, asked, 'See something you like?'

The accent was Kensington muted. Let you know he had class but not pushing it. I said, 'You're a bit young.'

'How many gun dealers have you met?'

'Son . . . how many would I want to?'

He let it settle, then decided to take it lightly. Or else . . . shoot me?

'And how is the good doctor?'

'Keeping well. Keeping stum more like.'

'Some refreshments?'

'Whatever.'

'Let us then to the penthouse.'

He wasn't kidding. Upstairs was the Heal's catalogue come to life. I liked it a lot, said, 'I like this a lot.'

He locked eyes, weighed the consequences then went for it, 'Killer.'

I settled in a couch that had the personality of a hypnotist, whisperin', 'Sleep, you're getting drowsier and drowsier.' Joseph said, 'I have some vodka here, has the personal approval of Yeltsin, thus quality.'

'I thought he went for quantity but yeah, give us a belt of that.'

He did, then, 'Yasseu.'

'Only yesterday I despatched a beautiful Ruger SP-101, a true work of art.'

I didn't know if regret or admiration was expected so I gave neither. Concentrated on the drink, it tasted cool and cold, a gentle kick that promised endurance. Mostly what it was like was more – lots and lots.

Joseph asked, 'Are you familiar with,

"if I have seen further than other men
it is because I have stood on
the shoulders of giants"

– know it?'

'Ran it by a mate only the other Tuesday.'

'Like some of my merchandise, I have modified it, thus:

"it's because I have sold to
the baseness of greed." '

I drained the vodka, got down the last tinkle and said, 'Fascinating and I'm sure you have a whole bunch of other quotes but, hey, let's get to the guns – OK, how would that be.'

He stood and I don't think he was well pleased.

'I thought perhaps you were a fellow traveller, that through the instruments of destruction we could comprehend transcendence.'

'Shit Joe, I have problems on the Northern Line – transcend that.'

So we weren't going to be buddies, especially not asshole ones. He left the room and didn't return for about twenty minutes. I nearly had a nap. Carrying two large flat cases, he opened them on the floor, began to pile out weapons, reciting, 'You've got your Glock, lightweight, plastic, undetectable by airport technology, a Baretta nine millimetre Parabellum, small wars model, a Colt, the basic western gun, looks serious. The Detective Special, beloved of Special Branch, makes them feel like movie stars.

'This big chappie is a Mark V1 Enfield. Yes, your assumption's correct, from those good folk who brought us the Lee Enfield and World War One. A variety of Mausers, very efficient. Uzis of course and, I have stocks of CS Gas, so popular lately.'

He had a light perspiration on his forehead and I realised – 'Jeez, this guy's hot for them'. He said, 'No need to rush. I'll leave you alone and let you get acquainted. Standard items such as 12-gauge and Brownings I keep downstairs. Enjoy!'

I fiddled about with them, did a few movie poses, dropped to combat position and generally clowned around. I gathered he'd be watching so, wot the hell, give 'em a show. When he came back, I was seated quietly and I said, 'The stage is BUR.'

'I beg your pardon?'

'El has left the building? No sweat, forget it.'

'You've made your selection.'

'Indeed I have. Have you got a pump shotgun, double loader.'

He was dismayed, spread his arms out, said, 'You don't wish any of these pieces?'

'Naw.'

Jeez, was he pleased, bundled up the gear with sighs and tut-tutting. I could give a fuck. Went and got me the pump and two dozen shells. Said in a sarcastic tone, 'I trust this is sufficient.'

'Yo Joseph, don't trust so easily eh. Tell you what though, if I run out, I'll give you a bell.'

I was handing over the wad of money as I said this. He paused mid-note, said, 'Oh, I don't think so. One feels a car boot sale would answer your requirements.'

I wasn't offended, offered, 'You ever in the market for a car yerself, give me a shout.'

'I very much doubt that Sir. I can't ever picture myself in the market for whatever it is you hustle.'

As he let me out, I tapped his arm, said, 'If I'm ever throwing a party, a wild one, you're top of my A-list pal cos fuckit, you're just a fun fella.'

He shut the door.

MOROCCO AND POINTS SOUTH

[illegible]

I [illegible] before the [illegible] was out [illegible] over the [illegible] I [illegible] enjoyed that [illegible] her on the [illegible] with [illegible] mopped her brow. She was wearing [illegible] and [illegible] Sure [illegible] and [illegible]

[illegible]

[illegible] because [illegible] I [illegible] to get [illegible] something [illegible] hear me coming and [illegible]

I didn't know what to make of this [illegible] So I asked, 'Can I [illegible] something?'

'Say what?'

[illegible]

'Coffee'd be [illegible] I had a little [illegible] I lived in New York City [illegible] name was [illegible] I loved her more than I thought I [illegible] hear. She filled [illegible]

[illegible]

[illegible] her [illegible] I [illegible]

Got home and shit, I was tired. Weapons and funerals, they'll do for you every time. Out of the car, gave the yuppie 'ping' and turned to my door.

Cassie literally materialised before me, staggered and I barely caught her before she hit the ground. She was out cold. Carried her over the threshold – yeah, I bet she enjoyed that – and laid her on the settee. Doused a cloth with ice water and mopped her brow. She was wearing late-evening hooker ensemble. Black bomber jacket, white and tight T-shirt, short black skirt, black stockings. Sure, the obvious crossed my mind but I tried to ignore it. She came round with little groans and whimpers, not unlike the sounds she'd made when we had sex. I asked, 'Are you OK?'

'Osteoporosis.'

'Excuse me?'

'Brittle bone disease, ain't it a bitch. Usually connected to the menopause but I had to get it early. I'll be literally cracking up – they'll hear me coming, and going.'

I didn't know what to make of this. More lies? So I asked, 'Can I get you something?'

'Say what?'

'Tea – a drink.'

'Coffee'd be good. I had a little girl, back when I lived in New York City. Her name was Ariana. I loved her more than I thought I could bear. She filled me with joy and wonder and pain and oh God, with yearning. I had to leave her alone for a few hours one evening – it's a long story why – when I got back, she was gone. I've never seen her since – that's partly why I'm such a goddamn mess.'

I agreed about her being a bloody mess but felt maybe it wasn't the time to mention it. Coffee, yeah, I was glad of the diversion. Made it hot and ball-bustin' strong. Elephant blend, as a mate said. At first I couldn't believe what I was hearing. Reckoned the Yeltsin had finally kicked in but no – she was singing! In a low clear voice of nigh absolute purity. I dunno about beauty, fuck knows, where would I have learnt, I was raised with pigeons. But, I'd bet this was close. I didn't know then but it was a song by Tricia Yearwood called 'O Mexico'. It had a ring of loneliness, of longing that hit like a gut-shot. I felt as close to weeping as a hard-ass like me's ever gonna come.

Then she stopped and the silence scalded my heart, muttered, 'Get a friggin' grip.'

I was wrung as tight as tension, not worth tuppence. If the filth had come callin', I'd have put up my hand, shouted – 'fair cop guv'. Carried out the coffee, no bizzies, Noble had scoffed the lot. She'd been crying, I wish I didn't know that and she said, 'Are you familiar with Thomas Merton?'

'Not unless he's a bookie.'

She quoted:

'We must be true inside
true to ourselves
before we can know
a truth
that is outside us.'

I poured the coffee, asked, 'How d'ya take it.'

'Cream and sugar –

"But we make
ourselves true by
manifesting the truth
as we see it." '

I handed her a mug, wondering if she'd finished. She had.

I took a sip, real good – fuck, I make great coffee.

'So Cassie, where's my gun . . . eh?'

'I tossed it.'

'You wot.'

'I was scared – scared I'd eat the metal so, I walked over Waterloo Bridge and sank the sucker. Is that the one Ray Davies wrote about – I saw the Kinks once.'

'And my money, I suppose you, dumped that too.'

'Don't be a horse's ass, I spent it, you've mucho dinero.'

'But not so mucho patience lady and your meter's running high. Lemme see if I can get this across. You stole from me, broke in to my gaff, took a shot at me and generally ran fuckin' liberties. Am I getting through to you Cassie. Our firm has been moving rag-ass trying to find you.'

'I've been naughty!'

'Naughty?'

'I need spanking.'

'Whoa – hold the phones lady.'

She was up, took my hand and put it on her breast, said, 'Hold this.'

I pushed her away and her voice dropped to a whisper.

'You don't want me?'

'Look Cassie, you're a hot lady but this isn't a real good time – OK.'

'It's because I lost my little girl, isn't it. You're punishing me.'

I stood up, 'For heaven's sake, I'm real sorry about that.

I'm trying to be fair, I'm not going to hassle you about all the other crazy shit. Just leave now and we'll let it be.'

'I think I see her, you know, on the street and I chase after her – or on a bus – or . . .'

'Jesus.'

'But I have a good report that she's in Agadir.'

'Where?'

'Morocco. Her father was from Kif.'

'I thought that was Keith Richards' nickname.'

'It's a village in the Blue Atlas Mountains, they specialize in hash. I know he now lives in Agadir, a P.I. says he's ninety percent sure.'

'A private investigator?'

'Yes, I've had dozens of them. Will you come – will you come and help me get her back.'

'I don't believe this. You can't just go down there on a vague report – can't you get Interpol to check.'

Her voice rose, 'Those pricks – do me a goddamn favour. But you're different, you'd get her.'

'I'm sorry, look it's late . . .'

'We could drive on down there, to Algeciras, I'd read MacNeice to you, I . . .'

'Stop it! Just stop it all to hell. You need help, but not any kind I can provide.'

Now she dropped her arms, seemed to shrink.

I took her arm, moved her to the door, opened it and had to push her out. She stood outside, like little Orphan Annie, said, 'You'll come to Agadir, you just don't know it yet but, I promise you that – on my little girl's head.'

I closed the door, said, 'Dream on lady.'

She stood outside the door and I could hear her say, 'David – David, did you ever hear what Kafka said,

"No people sing with such
pure voices

as those who live in
deepest hell." '

'Indigent! I don't friggin' believe it. You've got to be bloody joking – c'mon!' – Yelling at the very height of my lungs.

Doc took it all, well, almost, and replied, 'Would I joke about that. It's the term they use and a right vicious one.'

I couldn't take it in – how could he be *skint*—

'How can you be skint?'

'Don't get righteous with me Davy boy. The bloody house is mortgaged to the gills, those school fees – like murder – and the blackjack. It's been a long run of shitty luck, I'm going to have to pack it in.'

'Blackjack! You've been gambling – you've been wot? Why didn't I know?'

He stood up, his boots gleaming in the light, 'Why should you know. My bloody Missis didn't know. Since when do I account to you fella?'

I was close to losing it, had to pull back. I could see a roof in Battersea, see my father's eyes.

'OK . . . OK Doc. Might I ask how you propose paying for the Taj Mahal or whatever bloody monument you're building to Laura. Won't Father what's his bloody face be a tad surprised to hear you're – indigent – or does he play blackjack too?'

'Watch yer lip boy.'

'Or wot Doc?'

He made the effort also to rein in. We'd never – ever – hit this place before.

'Father Cleary doesn't know, alright. Treesmead will pay for his project and get me out of the hole – it has to.'

He paused, then, 'I went to see Meryl Streep in her action pic, *River Wild* and jeez, she was louder than the friggin' rapids, so my head was opening. Could you then stop shouting at me now – OK.'

I didn't even know I had been, said, 'I wasn't shouting – you went to the cinema without Laura.'

'Would have been hard to bloody bring her.'

I went to make coffee, brewed up a storm, heard Doc say, 'Tea for me, two sugars.'

Mutterin' 'Now he tells me' I half mangled a tea bag into a cup, sloshed water on it, tepid water. Put the sugar in before extracting the bag and, worst crime of all, didn't heat the cup. All petulant I grant you but it was that or reach for the new 12″, give it an early outing. Piled the lot on a tray that had Charles and Di's wedding portrait. As he sipped the tea, he gave a grimace, asked, 'Did you heat the cup?'

'Always.'

'Not yer best mate – no, not at all.'

'Doc, why don't I do this – I'll move some of the repo money to help you out.'

He gave a sheepish grin, 'Em . . . might be a slight problem.'

'No, I'll tell the accountant to do it – he gets paid to shuffle figures. A little cosmetic arithmetic and you're whistlin' Danny Boy.'

'I've been and sang that song already, 'tis not a tune worth humming.'

Now I was up, 'You've been dippin? You've been robbin *us*!'

'Whoa – slow down Streep. I'll put it back, it was just sitting there. But I do have good news.'

'You shot the accountant?'

He laughed, said, 'That's more like it son. Let me put it this way, Quinn won't be a problem, I know you were concerned there.'

'Jeez, you didn't top a cop!'

'Naw, they just broke his legs. If I'd another few hundred they'd have completed the job. But fuck, the readies are tight. Anyroad he won't be playing for the Police Reserves this season.'

'You're a piece of work Doc, you're a real fuckin' class act. I better buy a lorry load of strawberry delights.'

'What?'

'For the Noble savage, he's fond of his bikky he is.'

When Doc had gone, I thought about funerals. The way things were shaping, I'd soon be arranging my own. In prison, Doc had waxed eloquent and long about the Irish rituals for it, mainly he'd waxed long.

At a loss after Doc left, I flicked through the paper. Read an article on Patricia Highsmith and liked her saying, 'I find the public passion for justice quite boring and artificial, for neither life nor nature cares if justice is ever done or not.'

'Amen,' I said.

Time to move, I'd an accountant to see, Doc and I had force back-pedalled from out and out war. Not so much a sheathing of weapons as an option for other battlefields. But that didn't mean I couldn't bounce somebody's head off a wall.

Heard the post come through the box, didn't think it would be news to cheer. The handwriting on the envelope was now familiar. Could be worse I thought, the loony bitch could be phoning. Opened it with a heavy heart. In large clear writing she began,

'O Happi-Mou,

Why do you refuse us, we are destined to be one and, so it shall be. Time to wake up and smell that coffee – you hear what I'm saying.

A woman described my beloved MacNeice as having the looks of a fallen angel. Like you, he believed himself to have become, as a result of his childhood 'in a strange way hollow'. And he remained 'always terrified of his father'.

Darling David, let me make you complete. Ariana can be your daughter too. I just know you're made to be my family.

I won't be sending any more mail as, obviously, you won't be able to receive it. Don't fret about a suitable ardrobe for Morocco. I'll take care of all your needs. Men are hopeless at such practicalities. Feel the warmth touch your hand, that's me.

Sagapoh,
Your Cassie,
Siempre.'

I bundled it fast, lobbed and caught it on the fall with my right foot. Kicked it mightily across the room and saw it bounce off the far wall.

'In one,' I said.

I parcelled up the guns lest Noble came calling. Took them out to the car, piled them in the boot – a day to drive carefully. Thought I wasn't showing the strain till I got to the accountant's office and Iris said, 'What happened to you?'

'More important, what happened to Duran Duran?'

'You look rough Cooper, maybe you should call round to me, I'll give you some T.L.C.'

Time to cut to the chase.

'Is he in?'

'He's tied up.'

'Sure.'

And I barged on in.

He looked more like a sour priest than ever. A large slice of Danish was en route to his mouth, I said, 'Arnold L. White – mid bite.'

'What happened to knocking Mr Cooper?'

'What happened to my business?'

He took a chunk of the pastry, chewed a bit, then a gulp of coffee, replied, 'A touch of poetic justice you'll appreciate. Your firm is up for repossession – isn't that ironic.'

'It's fuckin' criminal is what it is.'

'You sound, how should I put it – surprised.'

'I'm bloody flabbergasted.'

'Am I to believe your partner didn't inform you of the developments?'

'Got that right pal. You didn't think to give me a bell yourself?'

'Not my place dear boy.'

'Leopold, don't you care if you go down the shitter with me.'

'Never happen Sir – I took precautions.'

I wanted to pound him, asked, 'What do you suggest I do now?'

'Run.'

'This amuses you, doesn't it. OK, gloat while you can but keep hoping I run far.'

'When you dallied with Iris, you did me a grievous injury.'

I turned to leave, left him with, 'Nice term that – grievous injury – has the proper note of righteous pain. What's more, I'm going to run it by you when I feed you your balls at a date to be arranged. Might I add, you can *count* on it.'

First I went to the lock-up. It doubles as a bolt hole – got bunk, kettle, shower, phone. All the vitals. Phoned Jimmy, he's a minor burglar I met in prison, he'd told me, 'There are some things a man *won't* do for money. Luckily, I'm not one of those men.'

He had the form to prove it.

'Jimmy?'

'Yeah.'

'It's Cooper.'

'The Repo Man.'

'Yeah, that too. Like to knock down a few hundred?'

'You want me to nick somefin.'

'Actually, I want you to add something. If I give you the guy's name, could you find his gaff and hide an item there.'

'Bit unusual, is this on the up an' up?'

'How does four hundred sound?'

'What's his name?'

I met Jimmy in the bar at Victoria Station. He arrived in a natty three-piece suit, hair spit-combed and I'd swear a regimental tie, said, 'Looking good Jimbo.'

'I've been taking lessons.'

'Is that a regiment tie?'

'Sure is – the Argylls – or is it the Enniskillens, one of those bods.'

'Why?'

'Opens a lot of doors.'

'You're the best judge of that.'

'I have a Masonic one too but, I have to be careful, I've never quite mastered the handshake. Is it a Mason or a Jesse, you know, a fella who's very friendly.'

Jimmy was smoking roll-ups, Old Holborn and, like a true con, he was a master. He offered, 'Smoke?'

'Naw. Here's the papers I want you to conçeal. Put them

in an obvious place but not so's the guy living there will find them – as if they'd been hidden.'

'Putting someone in the frame or is it none of my business?'

'It's none of your business. Here's the name and his work address. Any problems.'

'Any cash.'

'In the envelope. Do you know any hookers?'

'C'mon Cooper, go into any phone kiosk. Those cards there – take yer pick.'

'I need one who can keep her mouth shut.'

'That's a contradiction Cooper. The two don't gell – know wot I mean?'

'Cut the comedy eh – yes or no?'

'There's Sharon, she could do with a few quid. Here's her address, tell her you're my pal.'

'Right. You won't feel the urge to blab about our little transaction?'

'Aw, for God's sake, I'm a pro.'

'And you're healthy – best to remain so.'

'I'm a bit offended Cooper.'

'That'll pass, two broken legs would take longer.'

And then, I'd swear I saw Cassie on the upper floor. Jimmy said, 'You OK.'

But then she was gone.

'Yeah, thought I saw someone I knew.'

'You know wot they say, sit here long enough, you'll see everyone you ever knew.'

'I'm afraid you might be right – take care.'

'Or heavy weapons, am I correct.'

'Keep it in mind . . . later.'

I went into Burger King, ordered a whopper and a giant coke. Get the killing junk full in my stomach. Asked the guy to leave out the sauce and, of course, the burger came shitpiled with it. I was about to go through the routine when I saw David Letterman watching me. You know, the talk show, I'd been getting it on the late-night cable. Course it wasn't him but wow, a dead ringer. He smiled and I shrugged, wot else. Found a table where he wasn't in my line of vision. Bit down on the whopper and, sure as Sundays, the sauce shot out the side. Looked up, there he was, smile in place, said, 'I had you going, you did a double take.'

'Yank accent – jeez, another one.'

He said, 'The way I see it – he looks like me. Am I right?'

Took a hit of the coke and it was sweet, I'll give it that, even the ice.

'Might I sit down – I'm Cassie's brother.'

I finished the food, pushed the debris away, said, 'You're here for the shoplifting, I believe the season's started.'

'I need your help.'

'What's your name?'

'Let's call me David.'

'Wot – all of us?'

'Mr Cooper – oh yes, I know who you are. You may be the only one who can help her.'

'Sorry pal, I'm up to me arse in aggravation, plus – no offence but that lady's beyond help.'

'No no no! She's obsessed with you and you can use that to persuade her to return home. We can get treatment.'

'Hey David, you deaf or just stupid. I said – I didn't say – hey maybe we've room to negotiate.'

'I know where you're coming from Mr Cooper. But it's not a choice thing, she's volatile and, OK, I'm going to play straight with you. I believe she may have pushed a woman under a train in New York.'

'What . . . jeez . . . Laura . . .'

'Laura? Who's that? The woman was my fiancée. Cassie

doesn't like people close to her – loved ones – she doesn't share.'

I couldn't take it in. What was running through my mind was this family who looked like stars – Letterman and Sarah Miles. I asked, 'Who do yer parents resemble – Bogie and Bacall?'

And he laughed. 'They're Mom and Pop Diner, Mr and Mrs Ordinary, Citizens of Nerd City. You getting this?'

The door of the restaurant was kicked in, the three Yahoos came dribblin'. In their late twenties, they'd the uniform of denim jackets, combat trousers, scarves and filthy trainers. If grunge was gone, they hadn't heard. The personification of the urban hooligan to be found on every High Street, more common than litter and as nasty as tax. Intimidation is the party tune. Amid guffaws, obscenities and horseplay, they collected their grub and sprawled at the table next to us.

Naturally. This is your life! I said, 'The ambience at Burger King isn't to their palate.'

And now began the obligatory food fight, flicking fries and buns all over. He said, 'Gotta hang a right.'

And was up and over to them. He put both hands, palms outspread on their table. This put a thug to his left, to his right, and directly facing him. His accent seemed like a roar.

'Hi guys.'

'Wotcha want fooker . . . Yank fooker.'

Course this led to a wild repartee and chorus.

'Yeah, the fook you want wanker.'

'Are you guys the real thing – lager louts' (he pronounced it lowts) – 'we've got broadcasts on you back home.'

'Fook off wanker – put me shoe in yer arsehole – how d'ya like that then eh. Want yer fookin' teeth up yer backside, yah wanker?'

He stood back, gave a huge smile and charaded a light bulb going off over his head, answered, 'I know that word – you guys are implying I'm a self-abuser – have I got it right? But let me demonstrate what it is I actually do with my hands, OK?'

He bent slightly, then shot out both elbows to crash into noses left and right, then gave a bounce, gripped the table and headbutted number three. The sound of bones crackin' was loud. He pulled back and came over to me, asked, 'How'd I do?'

'Lemme put it this way – can I buy you a drink.'

As we got out of there, a round of applause followed us. I'd say it did wonders for Letterman's ratings.

We went to The Swan on Bayswater Road. I wanted away from my own manor. I ordered Scotch and he had Scotch rocks. I asked, 'You've got some moves, where'd you learn 'em?'

'Marine Corps.'

But he was staring at the painting behind the bar and the barman said, 'This pub has been here since Bayswater Road was a lane leading from the Courts in Uxbridge to Marble Arch.'

When David showed no recognition, the guy continued, 'Marble Arch, or as it was then, Tyburn, where they hung 'em! The condemned man and his escort would have a final drink here. See, that's what the painting shows.'

'One for the road.'

The barman gave a sour laugh.

'Didn't have to worry about being over the limit, know wot I mean.'

David looked him full in the face, said, 'I believe I catch your drift.'

Enough with the history I thought and moved us to a table, said, 'Cheers.'

'Whatever.'

'So David, what do you do?'

'I'm a poet.'

'Wot?'

'Ever listen to Stevie Nicks?'

'Not unless it's absolutely unavoidable.'

'She said – "they are poets of nothingness".'

'Are you any good?'

'Well, there isn't anyone good enough to know if I'm hot or not.'

'You should meet the Doc, he'd know. But a poet – bit like being a shepherd in London.'

He took out a pack of Camels, a Zippo, cranked it, blew out a batch of smoke, coughed, said, 'Hits the goddamn spot I think.'

'I thought Americans were violently anti-nicotine.'

'I like one of your writers, the Martin Amis guy, one of his characters wants a cigarette even when he's smoking one.'

'Sounds like madness to me.'

'Hey, what I did say – I said I was a poet – did you hear me say I was sane, did I run that by you. Amis reckons cigarettes are a relaxant and writers are the great un-relaxed.'

'David, I could give a toss whether you smoke through your arse.'

'Whoa, testy – I'm only making conversation here, OK.'

'What about yer sister, wot am I to . . .?'

'Lemme play a hunch here – you did her a good turn?'

He laughed loud, said, 'I imagine John Dillinger said similar as he walked outa the Bijou Theatre and into the guns.'

'I'm not Dillinger.'

'And heavens-to-Betsie, neither was Warren Oates but go figure. I made a shit-pile of bucks back in the manic '80s when Ginko was hoodwinkin' Wall Street. But heck, what have I got to show for it – a crazy sister, some property, and a heap of bad poetry.'

'You'd be different poor?'

'I probably wouldn't admit to the poetry. Next time she gets in touch – and she will – call me, any hour. Hell, call anyway, how would that be. Here's my card.'

'Aston Towers.'

'Yeah, impressive huh?'

As we left, he said, 'My old man, he was like . . . fifty-five when they had me. Yeah, on his deathbed he said, "Sorry I was old." '

I didn't know how to respond so I said, 'Just like my old man.'

'He said the same?'

'No, he said . . . Argh . . .'

Thought of something, then thought . . . check it out. Called, 'Em . . . David . . . Dave, wait up.'

Calling your own name, you feel like a horse's ass. He had the same thought as he answered in a high-pitched voice, 'Yes David.'

Shades of Tiny Tim and other obscenities.

'Cassie's daughter, wot's the story.'

He shook his head. Not good, said, 'There is no daughter. She had an abortion when she was nineteen . . . a botched job. After, she began exhibiting signs of psychosis. Then she invented a daughter and to explain her absence, she added abduction, not by aliens but Moroccans. Hardly an X-File but certainly spooky.'

I said more to meself, 'No Ariana.'

He gave me a playful puck to my shoulder. Jesus, I loved that! And said, 'No more eagles either but is that really such a bad thing.'

I said, 'She needs help.'

'Yo . . . Mister Cooper . . . didn't I just run that by you . . . didn't I just goddamn park in that space . . . pay attention . . . alright.'

And then he was gone.

Of all the things I was doing then, paying attention was definitely not one of them.

I didn't head for home till late in the evening. Turning from Clapham Road, coming along Ashmole Estate, I saw the fire engines. The entrance to my street was cordoned off but I could see the blaze clearly. My house was in full flame and I thought, 'Jeez, lucky I removed the guns and ammunition else it'd have taken out at least three firemen.'

I parked and walked towards the police line. A cop said, 'No passage here Sir, please go round.'

'That's my home.'

Standing a piece further down was Noble, the flames reflecting off his face, making it glow. He was wearing the grubby raincoat, turned to greet me, 'Mr Cooper, come through.'

As if I had a choice. He said, 'What rotten luck eh, the decorators are hardly out the door. You're covered I presume.'

'With wot?'

'Insurance man! Good heavens, you are insured?'

'Of course, I'm a citizen.'

'You'll be devastated all the same, I can read it in your face.'

His smirk was blatant.

'As long as it gives heat to the neighbours, can we really call it a total loss.'

He took my arm, whispered, 'It's too early to say for sure but it might be deliberate.'

I shook his hand off, said, 'Don't be daft.'

'Ah Mr Cooper, I have many shortcomings, that's not one I'm prone to.'

'Who'd torch my house, Noble.'

'I was hoping you'd answer that.'

'No idea.'

'I must say I admire your stoicism. Most people, they'd be in a highly emotional state.'

'I must be in shock, wouldn't you say. Drawing on your vast well of human experience, don't you think.'

'But the basics. Where will you stay?'

'Don't worry about me Noble.'

He moved right into my face, I could smell mints, 'But I do – you're almost family, what with the amount of time I think about you.'

'I'm touched.'

'And if not now, you will be. You'll be sorry to hear our Sergeant Quinn had an accident. Come now Mr Cooper, you can't have forgotten him. I know he thinks of you, if not fondly, at least persistently.'

'Car accident was it?'

'Sporting mishap actually.'

'What?'

'Yeah, two sports with baseball bats did a number on his legs. What you might term – a bad break.'

'I didn't reply but he read my face, said, 'Ah, you think I'm being facetious . . . no. You can tell me, strictly off the record, man to man.'

'OK – I think you're a prick and a bad bastard to boot. Being a cop you've been trained to it but, I think you were born a nasty piece of work.'

He was delighted, leastways his face was all lit up, answered, 'Good, excellent. I relish frankness and let me reciprocate. I've checked up on you, did yer stretch for GBH, a hard man. But I'm gonna have you Cooper, oh yeah. You took out the wrong cop, I'm not so easy.'

'Hey shithead, if I went after Quinn, I wouldn't need help.'

'See, yer hard like I said. Near time for you to go travellin' – yer mate has fucked yer business, yer home is gone . . . oh yes, and I'll be there, count on it.'

I pushed him aside, said, 'I hope that's a promise.'

And walked away. I didn't look at my ex-house, I could feel the heat. Went to the pub and ignored Lisa's barrage of questions, 'Was that your house! . . .'

Got a large Scotch and a corner to sulk.

No way in the world did I believe the fire was an Act of God. Course, I knew He was capable, the evidence was my life but I didn't think He could be bothered. I tried to remember what Cassie had said in her letter, something about no longer writing to me at that address as I wouldn't be able to receive mail. Exhibit A for the prosecution, pretty damning. Plus, she was a total friggin' nutter. Then there was the cops. Capable of anything but I wasn't convinced. Arson seemed a tad extreme when they'd countless methods to put me in the frame. The jury was out on them. The third possibility was the worst, I really didn't want to even consider it. Doc.

Ruthless and reckless enough to urge on my doubts about the bank job. He sure needed the cash and, if I had a similar motivation? Yeah, it was possible. I took a long belt of the Scotch and thought about Cassie pushing Laura under the train. Jeez, if Doc knew I was indirectly responsible – fuck, I'd have to shelve that.

I heard, 'You have the appearance of a man with a new lease of apathy.'

Think of the Doc and the devil appears, or something to that effect. I said, 'Very quotable, almost deep.'

'But not me own. Samuel Beckett it was, but at least 'tis the same country. What's all this about a fire?'

'Didn't take long to reach you Doc.'

'And aren't you my best mate, curled up in a corner like a whipped dog. Sure they had to call me.'

'Things are going down the shitter and fast.'

'You'll come home with me.'

'No . . . no, I don't think that's too clever. Noble's on the prowl and why make it easy for the bastard.'

'Ah don't mind him, the scut, he's like a boy whistlin' in the dark.'

'He's about to blow the flamin' whistle on me.'

Doc pushed in beside me, put his arm on my shoulder, said, 'Coop, listen boyo, they still need the oul reliable called evidence and there's not a bit of it. C'mon, I'll buy you a pint.'

'I've got to go. I'll be in touch tomorrow, we'll finalise the job details, OK.'

He gave me a worried look, 'Are yah up to it? I mean, have yah the stomach for it now?'

'Yeah, but the point is, do I want to. What worries me is Noble has minty breath.'

'So bloody wot?'

'A man who chews mints is an observer. They miss nothing and their agenda is not what's on display.'

''Ary, you're reading too much into it. He's probably covering up the smell of booze.'

I stopped into the 7-Eleven and stocked up on essentials – toothpaste, coffee, milk, soap – siege supplies.

I'd decided to crash in the warehouse for a few days, let the dust settle. Prison teaches you to move in small spaces, to need almost nothing. Before settling on the army cot, I rang Letterman.

'Yo – talk to me.'

'David, it's Cooper.'

'What's happenin' bro'?'

'My home's been burned.'
'And you wanna know is it Cassie, am I right.'
'There are other candidates, would she risk that.'
'Oh yeah . . .'
'How do I go about finding her?'
'She'll find you when she's ready for the next stage.'
'Fuck.'
'That too.'
'OK, I'll keep in touch.'
'Adios amigo.'

Next morning I woke with an aching back and couldn't figure where I was, said, 'Jeez, where am I.'

The warehouse looked like shit and I complemented it. Course I'd no razor and the electric kettle went on the blink. Took a cold shower and froze my balls off. Invigorating, they say, which is not the term that sprang instantly to mind. And, I'd need clothes, not to mention a whole new life.

Sat and wrote out the hooker manifesto, had to word it just right. Then rang the number Jim had given me. She was home and arranged a meet for three in the afternoon. Next up was the bank, to withdraw a shit-pile of money. The cashier looked worried but then, that's what they're paid for. She said, 'Excuse me a moment.'

'Why?'

'I need verification.'

'Take my word for it, it's my money.'

She gave one of them banking smiles, all teeth and malice.

'It's a rather large amount.'

'No one said that when I lodged it.'

'I'll just be a sec.'

And off she went.

I looked round, professional interest. Maybe I'd return and do this one for spite, take a hop outa the cashier. Back she came with an older guy. He didn't have a sign that read,

'I mean business, very serious business
and I just know you're not it.'

But he had the look, said, 'If you'll step over here a minute Mr Cooper.'

I did . . . and waited. He began, 'Might I suggest with such a large amount that we consider other alternatives.'

'No.'

He faltered; then rallied, 'Of course Mr Cooper, any advice I can offer.'

'Give me the money.'

He did. I don't think my attitude had been covered in customer relations.

From there I went to the markets and bought three pairs of jeans, six shirts, three formal slacks, underwear, three pairs of shoes, and two hold-all jackets. Even at market prices, it burned a hole. Back to change and in the new gear I felt, if not renewed, at least ready. Said aloud, 'Let's burn a cop,' and picked up the phone. Got the number of Scotland Yard, dialled, asked for the serious crime division. Put on hold, then a gruff voice: 'Can I help?'

'I dunno, you might want to hear that a detective named Noble, outa Carter Street, was helping an accountant named Arnold L. White. Mr White has been behind the series of bank raids up and down the country.'

Silence. What did I expect . . . glee? When a cop is ratted out, they like it as much as duty in Brixton, then, 'And your name is . . .'

'Concerned Citizen.'

Snort!

Which sound seemed appropriate to hang up on. I didn't expect they'd rush out and nick Noble but, with the hooker's call later, I wanted to muddy the water. Give the bad fuck something to suck mints about.

My hands were wet from tension. I should have known that a call like that wasn't going to be simple. When they own you for two years, the automatic responses never fully fade. Like walking into a snake pit having previously been bitten and saying – 'it won't hurt so bad.' Dream on sucker.

Almost immediately the phone rang and I jumped – 'bloody hell,' they're on to me already?! Picked it up, said tentatively, 'Yeah.'

'David.'

'Cassie.'

'You recognised me lover, that's promising.'

'How'd you find me?'

'In the book.'

'Oh.'

'You met my brother.'

'Jeez, what is this – you have private investigators on me?'

'You've a high profile honey. So, has he been shooting you a line, telling you I'm whacko and stuff.'

'He's concerned – where are you?'

'I'm real close baby, but you get the hell away from him. You hear what I'm saying?'

'Or wot . . . you'll burn my house down . . .'

The line went dead.

The hooker, Sharon, lived at Waterloo. Those small houses near the bridge, like a real Coronation Street. Rang the bell and she answered immediately. In her mid-forties, she was a brunette with trowelled on make-up. Carrying weight that looked like it was going to increase and wearing a lurex tracksuit, she said, 'Jim's mate, right?'

'Yeah.'

'You seem disappointed, was I supposed to brassen up. I thought this was other biz, not a shag call.'

'Can I come in?'

'Sure darlin'.'

And she sounded like a hooker then. A husky voice that was only part fake. Led me into a living room, it looked cosy like a home and she noticed my approval, said, 'You were expectin' a bordello.'

'I expect very little.'

'Can I get you something – tea, a drink.'

'No . . . just a phone call. I have it written down, you just read it, I pay you and I'm gone.'

'You up to a little action?'

'Not today.'

'You're one of those men, don't pay for it . . . right?'

'Sharon, let's quit the analysis. You shut the fuck up, read the script and we're done, can you do that.'

'Let's do it.'

I handed her the sheet of paper, she read it but skipped comment. I gave her the number. Here's what she read: 'Metropolitan Police . . . yeah, can you put me on to the robbery division.'

She gave me a sick smile as she was put on hold, then, 'I have information regarding the country-wide bank jobs.'

Hold again. She clicked her fingers, indicated a pack of Major and matches. I loved those clickin' fingers but got her one and handed it to her. The phone was now nestling between her chin and shoulder, so beloved of broads in movies and busy folks everywhere, she hissed, 'The matches . . .'

Yeah.

I lit the cigarette and she drew dust from the very carpet. Her face contorted and was followed by a horrendous cough. One of those lungs to the roof of the mouth jobs. She spoke again. 'Let's say I was involved with one of the guys OK . . . yeah . . . fucked me over . . . get the picture. Hey, if you want to hear this or not . . . the proof?

Well, if you go to the flat of Arnold White, accountant, you'll find maps, diagrams, plans for all the jobs. The address? . . . wot, you want me to do all the bloody work, try detectin' it. White, you want me to spell it . . . No . . . not Leonard . . . A . . . R . . . N . . . O . . . L . . . D . . . yeah, I'll tell you how it works. These are the three big banks,

Barclays

Nat West

Lloyds

Yeah, in each of those, there is a clerk who supervises the transfer of large sums to provincial branches. Their names? . . . Detect them. They inform Mr White as to when and where. Yer cop Noble, he provides the data on local policing. Who and what to avoid. Course it's simple . . . why cha fink it works.

' – Yeah, up yours too.'

And she banged the phone down. I said. 'That went rather well, don't you think.'

Her face was enraged and she moved to a cupboard, took out a whopper-size bottle of vodka, one glass. Poured a shoot amount, knocked it back clean. I remembered the gun dealer, his Yeltsin brand. If it hit the spot, she didn't show it, said, 'I've been a lot of things in my sorry time but never a grass. I don't like the taste of it and I don't think I like you a whole lot better – know wot I mean.'

I counted out her money, all crisp new bills, asked, 'Do you like my new gear, only got it today.'

'Wot?'

'While you're "finking", lemme ask you this. When Jimmy told you about the job, did he say you'd have to like me, maybe we'd share sob stories, fight a little but eventually love would blossom? And we'd fade away to the Kinks playing in the background. Did he mention shit like that?'

'Wotcha on about, course he didn't!'

I stood, liked the way the new jacket hung – stylish but not blatant, said, 'So, shut yer bloody mouth. I also suggest you forget this whole incident. You're going to have to trust me on this but, you wouldn't want me to come back.'

I expected further cheek but instead, 'You're an only child, aren't you?'

'Excuse me?'

'I can always tell, you have that air of front and blackguardism.'

I liked that word, said, 'To tell you the truth Sharon, I asked my old Mum if I'd been adopted. She said she'd tried but no one would have me.'

She took the money, counted it and I thought . . . when the Doc told me that yarn everyone cracked up but perhaps my timing was off. As I left she was lifting the vodka.

As I turned towards Waterloo Bridge, Jimmy came out of a doorway. He was grinning, not a pretty sight. I said, 'This better be coincidence.'

'Don't be like that, I only wanted to make sure everything went smoothly. Iron out any problems, that's all – cross my heart, straight up.'

'It's good, I'm glad I met you here.'

'You are.'

'See . . . see that spot over there, that's where I near killed the mugger, you heard about it right . . . wot I went to the nick for.'

He backed off, not noticeably but a gradual edging away, I went with him, continued, 'I never told anyone this Jimmy, not a soul, but I want to tell you . . . fuckit, I need to tell someone . . .'

He was glancing round, avenues for escape. I slapped

my open right hand on his shoulder, said, 'Jim, I enjoyed it . . . but wait . . . hang a mo' . . . I want to do it again so badly . . . Know wot I mean?'

THE LAST CALL

And one ... great Bottom had ... a ... and ... ago. A ... in a ... I'd taken my ... him and he walloped me across my shoulders with his walking stick ... my ... had ... as I stumbled towards ... him ... with the ... stick. ... The girl was dead ... had to be ... to salvage ... who wants ...

... I ... we ... at ... met ... ... no more than ... in the bank seconds later. Now it had ... to shut. Doc gave ... and I roared. ... the ... money. He did.

Pulled ... the ... there, he'd been right ... depart ment. Looked more than ... ever ... we ... hadn't looked at ... either. I mean ... they'd ... it was an accident ... I didn't ... that's why I was ... only for ...

...

Both barrels in the cashier's face and the blast threw her from her till. I'd been holding the shotgun in her direction, Doc a few feet away was roarin', 'Everybody get the fuck down – *now.*'

And one of the great British traditions came to play – a bastard 'had a go'. A fuck in a blazer, near seventy. I'd taken my eyes off him and he walloped me across my shoulders with his walking stick – my fingers had squeezed the trigger as I stumbled forward. Doc leapt for him, clubbed him with the gun's stock. Now everyone was screaming. The girl was dead, had to be, so I thought I'd salvage something, shouted, 'Who's next . . . eh . . . who wants some more!'

And I cranked two shells in, let them see it.

Silence.

It had been going so well. The incendiaries Doc had planted at the cop shop, Tesco's and the Masonic Lodge went off in sequence. More noise than damage and we'd been in the bank seconds later. Now it had turned to shit. Doc gave me a look and I roared, 'Get the fuckin' money.'

He did.

Filled two bin-liners, he'd been right in that department. Looked more than we'd ever pulled but we hadn't looked at murder either. I mean . . . they'd believe it was an accident? . . . I didn't mean it M'Lud . . . honest – that's why I was carrying a 12-gauge, only for demonstration purposes. Yeah, a judge would understand. Good-night Irene. With good behaviour we'd be out in 2701.

As usual we'd two cars. Outside waiting was the 'borrowed' – a Vauxhall Tigre Coupe with automatic form. Our legit one was back at the Services Stop. A Volvo 850 GLT T5, the four-door saloon. Chosen purely for its top speed of 149 mph and the acceleration didn't hurt either – 0–622 mph in 74 seconds. I could vouch for that. Its beauty though – drop a couple of gears to bring the turbo on line, kick on the throttle and yer off. Meatloaf's 'Bat outa Hell' on yer tapedeck . . . eat fucking dust. I wished it was outside the bank. Our system was for Doc to now take my shooter, and double-armed he'd stand as I rushed to the car with the cash. It had always worked before. Seemed to again.

I slung the bags in back and shit, heard sirens, put the Coupe in gear. Doc came edging out slow, his back to me. A woman stepped from a doorway between us. Cassie!

Dressed in black, short bomber jacket and mini skirt, she took the pose beloved of movie posters. Feet apart, both hands on the pistol, ready to kick ass. Before I could react, she fired four times, taking Doc in the legs. He went down like an elephant, the shotguns sprawling uselessly. She turned, looked right at me and smiled, began to tighten her finger on the trigger. I hit the ignition, into gear and drove off. Near collided with a school bus and then I was outa Treesmead, going like a demented thing. My pounding near deafened me to all else and I kept shouting – 'get to the rest stop, get the Volvo . . . get, get, get . . .' – as if ritual would deliver me.

You ever see that movie *Predator* with Arnie. A character says, 'You lose it here, you're in a world of hurt.' I was living the line. Kris Kristofferson used to whine, 'Freedom's just another word for nothing left to lose' – as I gunned the Volvo I sang that. But some survival instinct forced a plan. In Sidcup I stopped, went into Boots and bought a pack of razors and the large rapid-tan. Next I got a large duffle bag. On form there. I pulled into a layby and with a reasonably steady hand, shaved my head then applied the tan all over it. By the time I hit London, I'd be orange, tanned or nicked. If you want to go to ground in London, Notting Hill Gate has a lot in its favour. The small Indian-run hotels are only interested in cash. Calling the police is not high on their priorities. There's a huge cosmopolitan floating population and, it wasn't my manor.

When I checked in, I looked like a brown Kojak. I didn't recognize me. First off I collapsed on the bed and slept for nigh twelve hours straight. If I dreamt I don't recall it and nor would I wish to. I'd given the manager a week's money up front and thus ensured, if not welcome, at least acceptance.

I came to with my heart hammering. For a moment I thought I was back in prison and as I realized where I was, relief chased terror to become anxiety. Crawled from the bed and moved to the small sink, it had a cracked mirror. Near coronary all over again as a bald brown head peered back . . . shouted – 'What the fuck?'

Had the french whore's bath, washing from the basin, then took stock. I'd need clothes, re-tanning, and a whole shit pile of luck. The hotel was in Coburn Gardens, off the main strip. It had a rundown sleaziness that fitted my appearance. I was on time for breakfast and was ready to hammer caffeine. A radio was playing as I entered the dining area – The Mavericks with 'It's a Crying Shame'. This fitted about every area of my life.

The room had six tables and I manoeuvred to an empty one. A young Indian girl asked, 'Tea or coffee?'

'Coffee please.'

Krishna bless her I thought as she brought a pot and two tough bread rolls. She eyed me warily and I guess my bullet head was responsible. There's something intrinsically psychotic about a shaved skull. I mean, even women look creepy when they're skin-scalped. Look at Sinead O'Connor!

I loosened some teeth on the bread rolls and horror! . . . stared at the white back of my hands. Fuck, I'd neglected to tan them. A guy in his fifties in a decrepit suit, sat, asked, 'Join you?'

'You already have.'

He extended his hand, 'Harris . . . in textiles . . . you?'

'In bits.'

'Excuse me.'

He had a north of England burr, unpleasant over brekkie and he said, 'I'm from up North lad, no work there, the Social popped me in here.'

'This is a welfare hotel?'

'Not all of it lad, they have some rooms for short-term emergencies. You're a seaman, am I right?'

'How astute.'

He got his rolls and made fast work of them, eyed mine, said, 'You'll be having them lad?'

'Hey, you want more, ask them.'

'Two per man, that's the regulations, don't want to rock the boat, if you'll excuse the pun.'

His face was a map of blackheads – some must have dated from his teens. I drank my coffee quickly. He said, 'There's a major change coming.'

'You wot?'

'To Notting Hill Gate. I've been reading up. Got to keep abreast of your surroundings, key to the top.'

I'd already had enough, time to cut him off at the knees, said, 'A code that's obviously stood you in good stead.'

Lost on him.

'You'll have seen Newcombe House, ugly place beside Waterstones.'

'Hard to miss.'

'Well, they're going to create small piazzas outside that . . . and Boots. They've plans for new benches, railings, and a hundred and thirty trees have been planted.'

I thought I'd plant him shortly.

'I let my housing officer know I was aware of these renovations.'

'Why?'

'To show I'm willing to be part of it, to live here. I'm attracted by the air of bohemia.'

I stood up but he didn't shut it.

'It used to be called Knottynghull.'

'Fascinating.'

And left him rambling.

I forced my mind to block out the image of the dead cashier. Jesus! And Doc going down like a shot bull. Think survival – think, think, think . . .

Out on the street I went to Oxfam, bought shirts, jeans and jackets. Left them off at the hotel, dressing down, dressing dead. Peeled off a thick wad of notes, headed out anew. Kept my eyes averted from the news-stands. Not up to that yet. Bought a walkman in W.H. Smith and picked up a heap of tapes in the Music & Video Exchange. The streets were jammed, every tongue spoken save English. Had to go to High Street Kensington to find a tanning centre. Booked an intensive week of sessions and the girl said I could be in right away. Strapped the walkman to my undies and lay on the sunbed, saying – 'bake me senseless'. It did.

Come outa there with my skin on fire. I'd played tapes and heard nothing, played them mega-blast and heard diddly. My mind fear-focused in Treesmead bank. Like prison, I got away from there but I'd never get free.

Chose a crowded pub, ordered a large Scotch, then asked, 'Got a paper?'

'Wotcha want, *Sun* or the *Guardian*?'

'Lemme have a look at both.'

Took them to a corner seat, did one swallow to the drink and let it hit, picked up the *Sun* wishing I smoked.

Staring back from the front page was myself and the headline, 'Mad Dog Shoots Two'.

Two!

This was the gist of the story: 'In a bloody raid yesterday, a crazed gunman killed a young cashier. For no apparent reason, he pushed a shotgun in her face and fired. He then shot his accomplice.'

Wot!

'Witnesses said the gunman wanted to kill everybody but was restrained by his partner. Lieutenant-Colonel Robert Foss (retired) tackled the vicious killer but was clubbed to the floor. The gunman then turned on his accomplice, shooting him at point-blank range. It's believed the man, though critical, will survive. Estimates for the haul put the amount taken in excess of half a million.'

My head was reeling and I got another double. Sank that, didn't help, read on, 'A massive police search was launched. They are anxious to interview David Cooper, a car dealer from Lambeth. The public are cautioned not to approach this man but to telephone the numbers given below.'

Put the paper aside, turned to the sports page. The photo of me was from my prison days, I hadn't looked like that in years. Swore under my breath. No one had seen Cassie – jeez, wot sort of luck did she have. Worse, the bastards figured I shot Doc . . . fuck, what if Doc believed that. I was way past shit creek.

Picked up the *Guardian*, same story but less sensation and only half the front page, same lousy photo. At least they weren't screaming 'Mad Dog'. On page three was a short column on the suspension of Chief Inspector Noble, pending investigation. Nothing on the accountant.

I left the pub and tried to tell myself the Scotch had jizzed me up. What I got was tired. Caught sight of myself in the huge window at C&A and didn't half throw a fright. A bald, baked psycho – then amended that to include the tag Rich-ish. I mean, it said so in the *Sun*.

For the next three days, I sizzled thru the tanning sessions, shaved my skull daily, ignored newspapers and slept like a dead thing. Walked . . . wow, did I ever – mile on mindless mile, all through Hyde Park. Watched the water at the Serpentine, read the hooker cards at Marble Arch, tried to formulate a plan.

I've always liked me grub. Doc said 'a meat and potatoes man', in every sense. When the cash was high, I'd do steak at least twice a week. Gimme one of them pepper jobs, pile on the roast spuds and I could imitate contentment. Other times I like the meat rare, see the juice flow on out. Or hit a mega breakfast – double sausage, bacon, puddin', and splash fried eggs all over. Convict's delight. Now, the very thought of any of that made me retch. I'd gone into MacDonalds, ordered a Big Mac and the sight of it made me throw up. I didn't need a psychologist to tell me why. Wouldn't the *Sun* love it – 'Mad Dog Goes Veggie'.

If this was the only price, I'd consider it light penance. I feared it was but a beginning – don't cry for me Treesmead. Yeah, like that. I checked the accommodation notices in the newsagents and liked the sound of this:

Room in quiet house for respectable
gent. Non-smoker preferred.

Situated just off Portobello Road, it was owned by a widow in her forties. A no-nonsense type, she'd rely on instinct not references, even her name was to the point – Mrs Blake. I said, 'Harris . . . in textiles . . . up North.'

And gave her the honest if dim expression. I got the room. Two huge bonuses, no other lodgers and no TV. She said, 'I don't hold with it.'

What else could I add but, 'Me neither.'

She'd provide breakfast and an evening meal on

Sunday – did I have any preference foodwise? I told her I was vegetarian and she asked, 'You're not some sort of new age traveller . . .?'

'No, no – my wife, before she died, couldn't take meat, so I tried to make it easier. After she passed away, I suppose it's silly, but I felt it would be disloyal.'

She put up her hand, 'You needn't say any more, I understand completely.'

I'd scored big but had to be careful I didn't overdo it. If she thought it was odd a Northerner had a London accent, she didn't say. I'd considered running the area's proposed developments by her and flourishing with Knuttyhill but decided not to play silly buggers. If I could get four to five days' avoidance of news reports, I'd not have to learn the cashier's name, age, home-life aspirations. I knew any details would lodge forever tormenting.

My old man was weather-tanned from being on the roof with the pigeons, he'd also lost his hair. As I sat in my new room the horrible realisation hit that I was now his spittin' image. The old adage – 'study your enemy well lest it's him you become'. Too late! Come full bloody circle to be him. If I'd known that in Battersea, I'd have gone off the roof too.

Walking towards Ladbroke Grove, my skin was settling into its colour and the Bruce Springsteen song 'Till The Light Of Day' was in my head.

I smiled as the words bounced on my soul but I'd learnt it's possible to survive within the darkness. If I could just step a little further . . . Yeah, time to rock 'n' roll.

From the repo business, I'd learnt where to get a car, to get it fast, cheap, and semi-legal. I headed for Ladbroke Grove. An Asian guy was running the yard, he'd some mileage himself and not due to age. The marks on his face were the remnants of an acid attack, one eye was closed. I tried not to stare, looked at the lot's drawing point – a white Bronco. He said, 'For the rapid mover.'

'Didn't move very rapid for O.J.'

'Ah see, since then . . . is very popular.'

I moved to an Aston Martin, liked its condition but he wouldn't budge from a ridiculous sum. Sure, I could afford it but I couldn't afford the attention. Instead, did a reasonable deal for a battered Mini and drove outa there. Even in that, it felt good to be mobile, almost in control.

Parked in Holland Square and went to a phone, took a while but eventually got Doc's priest. He said, 'Who is this?'

Jeez, I liked the note of petulance, how busy was the fuck. I said, 'This is Cooper.'

Silence . . . then, 'Where are you Mr Cooper?'

'Cornwall.'

'Well laddie, I suggest you hotfoot it to the nearest police station and give yourself up.'

'Did I ask for your advice Padre . . . how is Doc?'

'He's recovering – if such a thing is possible after such treachery. Thank God you're not an Irishman.'

'It's not how it seems. Tell Doc I'd never do that.'

'Really Mr Cooper, do you think I'm an eejit. I'm afraid Doc has had to give you up.'

'What!'

'He owes you nothing – I strongly advised him to do so.'

'Tell me Padre, do you still want the money . . .'

'The money . . .'

'Half a million quid, yer own little lottery win.'

'Em . . .'

'How would this be Padre – seeing as Doc is singing . . . why don't you try whistlin'. Yeah, fuckin' whistle real hard.'

Banged the phone down hoping I deafened him.

There's an Italian restaurant beside Holland Park famous for its pizza. I ordered a double cappuccino, no chocolate spread, I hate that. A woman was seated at the next table in full verbal to a young girl, 'It's true, the pill for men, can you imagine. As if there's a woman on the face of this earth who'd trust a man to take the responsibility. Oh yes dear, I'm on the pill, cross my heart, honest.'

I tuned her out. With her mouth, they'd need a pill that included deafness.

The phone had brought me way down. What did I expect. Doc was only doing to me what he believed I'd done to him. He was the only friend I ever had. If a friend could truly be the ideal, someone who believed in you despite the evidence of, jeez *because* of it. Holy Moley, wouldn't that be good. Dream on sucker.

I could take a stab at such nobility. Yeah, get the shrine built to Laura, pay the school fees for the daughter, make sure Doc had cash for his old age.

The cappuccino came, chocolate on top and I muttered 'fuck 'em'.

What I'd do was find Cassie. As I was leaving I gave the waiter a pound, he said, 'Ah *scuzi*, is not right.'

'Neither was the coffee so we're even.' Michael Caine in *Mona Lisa* used to say to Bob Hoskins, 'It's the little things George.' He had a point.

I went and did a further session on the sunbed. I was tanning deep and crispy. When I got back to my new accommodation, the landlady said, 'I do declare, you seem to get browner by the minute.'

I felt she was going to add . . . 'and balder'.

But discretion won out. Upstairs, I shaved yet again. I'd bought a watchman's cap, you know those wool jobs that pull down over yer ears and neck. By Christ, they're warm and just a tad off, like a mugger's outfit. Said . . . 'time to get armed' and drove through to Islington in the evening. Be nice to see the gun dealer again, he was such a ray of sunshine.

Parked near the green and strolled down. I was wearing jeans and a donkey jacket, Oxfam's finest – 'Auf Wiedersein Pet'.

Yeah.

At his door, I pulled the hat on, the less he'd remember the better. Knocked twice. The door opened almost immediately – he was wearing black ski pants, black sweatshirt with 'CATS' on the front, bare feet, I said, 'It's Cooper, Doc's friend.'

I heard all sorts of shit in prison. One thing Doc told me from his studies: 'If you experience deep shock, self-preservation moves into the go area and sometimes never climbs down again. It remains fixed on red alert.'
His smile did that to me now as he said, 'Come in . . .'

I thought . . . uh-uh.

We went to the luxury pad on the top floor and he asked, 'Drink?'

'Yeah, some of that Yeltsin stuff again.'

He moved to a sideboard behind me. I sat on the sofa, could hear the clink of glasses then spun round. He was just over me, a syringe in his right hand. I grabbed his wrist and used my other hand to clutch his hair, pulling him up and over. Shot my leg up as a pivot on his chest and used the leverage to fling him from me. Then I righted myself and moved to smack him twice in the mouth . . . all fight leaving him.

I said, 'Now look wot you've done, gone and got blood on CATS. You want to tell me wot the fuck you're at . . . I already had my shots.'

Pulled him into an upright position, grabbed his head and crashed his face with my knee. Heard the nose go – pushed him away. Blood was coursing down his face and I rummaged in his desk for tissues, found a handgun. The Glock, loaded, put it in my jacket. Gave him the tissues and poured two strong drinks. He'd gone into a crouch position and I said, 'Drink this.'

'My nose, it feels like a football.'

Let him get some booze and my heartbeat to settle, then asked, 'What kind of wanker are you? Enough guns here to arm the Met and you come at me with a needle! Like Sean Connery said in *The Untouchables* – "Trust a wop to bring a knife to a gunfight." You're not Italian are you?'

'It's for grasses, wot you give squealers, turncoats . . .'

'What's in it?'

'Smack . . . heroin.'

'And.'

'It's been cut with bleach.'

'Nice.'

'It's open season on you Cooper. Doc's friends put together a bounty on you. Even the Old Bill kicked in a contribution.'

I finished the drink, went over to him, took the Glock from my pocket, hefted it, testing the feel. No weight at all, like a plastic toy, asked, 'If you were me, things being how they are – what would you do? Would you use the syringe or this gun maybe.'

He had no suggestions so I added, 'Well, you think about it OK.'

I got outa there quick. As I headed for my car, I whipped the cap off . . . jeez, it sure itched. Was back in The Gate in under thirty minutes and that's impressive. Who could I tell? A shitload of fatigue hit me and I decided to call it a night. My landlady was nowhere in sight and I felt deeply grateful. Sometimes, even the tiniest social interactions are too much. Climbing into bed I put the Glock under my pillow. If they came for me, I was halfway ready. 'They' now seemed to comprise most of the population of London.

And dream? Did I ever – a mix of priests with sweatshirts saying 'CATS', Doc with a syringe and my father on a sunbed, a pigeon clutched to his chest. Tobe Hopper stuff. Woke with a saying of my mother's in my head:

> 'Men talk about sex
> Women talk about surgery.'

Shook myself to get free, muttering, 'No wonder he took to pigeons.' Put on the Oxfam jeans, found a coin in the pocket which meant A: I was getting lucky or B: Oxfam hadn't bothered their concerned ass to clean 'em. Next a sweatshirt with a hole in the sleeve, then a pair of weejuns, the real thing too. Put them on yer feet, you're in sole heaven. I felt weary though, thinking – getting older's getting harder.

Yeah.

Decided I'd nip up to a coffee shop at The Gate, kick start on a chain of espressos.

The landlady was waiting, said, 'I've brewed fresh tea, nice crisp toast.'

'Shit', I thought and said, 'Lovely job.'

Into the kitchen. A gingham tablecloth to match the curtains. The false reassurance of toast popping . . . to suggest endless possibilities. There wasn't a rose in a vase but the atmosphere whispered – 'close call'.

I sat and she fussed round doing kitcheny stuff, said, 'I nearly did a fry-up but remembered your vegetarianism in time – does it preclude eggs?'

'No, no, eggs are fine but not today, in fact any day with a yolk in 'em.'

She gave me a blank look and I added, 'Good of you to bother.'

'No trouble to tell you the truth.'

When you hear that statement, reach for your wallet or a weapon.

'It's nice to have someone to prepare for. Course you know wot it's like to lose someone.'

I sure as hell didn't want her story so bowed my head and she changed direction.

'Mind you, it's hard to picture you married.'

'Excuse me?'

As she struggled for words, I thought – yeah, I'm a liar, say it.

'You have the look of a single man, used to pleasing yerself. Married men have a more confined expression, as if they've suppressed a sigh for too long. It's not a criticism, only an observation.'

I wanted to say – psychology bloody one eh, but drank my tea, muttered, 'Laura was the world to me.'

It had the desired effect, her face took a wounded look.

'There I go again, me 'n my big mouth. My George used to say . . .'

'Is that the time, I'll have to run . . . thank you for the tea.'

I left her mid-sentence with whatever nugget of wisdom bloody George had bequeathed. I didn't think I'd short-changed myself. At Portobello Road a guy was shouting, 'Keep England for the English.' I remembered Nick Hornby saying in his football book, 'By the early seventies I had become an Englishman, that is to say I hated England just as much as half of my compatriots seemed to do.'

Well.

I'd finally got up with the Letterman Show and what I couldn't understand was – just wot was the fucker laughing at all the time. Rang the number, he answered immediately, the voice so like Cassie, 'Yo, talk to me.'

'It's Cooper.'

'No shit . . . the one-man crime wave. What's your beef buddy, I mean first you take out a cashier and then your partner. Are you nuts or what.'

'That's not exactly what happened.'

'Whatever you say buddy. You sure pulled in a shit-pile of greenbacks.'

'Can we meet?'

'But will I come away in one piece?'

'Of course.'

'Sure, I'll meet you buddy.'

'Thanks . . . thanks a lot. I'll be in the Magdela Tavern at nine tonight. That's in South Hill Park, NW3.'

'Whoa, hold the phones, lemme just get this down . . . okey-dokey. Why there, I'm gonna need my A–Z.'

'It's where Ruth Ellis caught up with Colin Blakeley.'

'You've lost me buddy.'

'The film *Dance with a Stranger*.'

'Miranda Richardson, right?'

'Exactly.'

'Well I'll see you there. Don't shoot anyone else . . . OK.'

And he rang off.

I hadn't told him Ruth Ellis waited outside the pub which is exactly what I planned. At least the waiting part, the rest would just have to be played out.

That evening I arranged the money in a suitcase, row by row of neat piles. I tried not to visualise the cashier. Snapped it shut and shoved it under the bed. If I didn't get back, the landlady would eventually find it. Would she give it up or leap for bloody joy . . . go find a new George.

Wore the donkey jacket again and put the Glock in the right-hand pocket, easy access. Dark jeans, shirt, and trainers, said, 'Cassie.'

I was parked outside the pub at eight forty-five. Letterman drove up at nine on the button in an Audi, parked recklessly and went into the bar. I estimated thirty minutes tops before he'd decide I wasn't coming. It took forty-five. He came stormin' out, got in the car and roared away.

He was easy to follow, an angry driver sees only his road. Aston Towers had the smell of money and he drove into a basement garage. I waited fifteen minutes then went to check the name bells. Rang the top one, a woman answered. I said, 'Pizza for the Trentons.'

They buzzed me in. I found the stairs, went to the first floor, knocked at a door, a voice said, 'Who is it?'

I took a breath then tried a loud Yank accent, 'David 'ol buddy, you ready or what.'

'You want 4B for Godsake.'

Not a sound in the place. Money buys quiet. Listened outside 4B, could hear nothing, rang, kept my face in profile. Letterman asked, 'What ya want?'

'Electrician.'

He threw the door open and I said, 'Our next guest is . . .'

Put the gun in his face and added, 'Let's take it inside.'

He backed slowly away from me into a living room. Cassie was lotus style in front of a huge TV, or is that yoga. Anyway with her legs folded, hands resting on her knees. Dressed in shorts and a halter top, for all the world like Sarah Miles at rest.

'Guess what . . . she turned up.'

'I can see that.'

'No, I mean like . . . today. Go figure huh . . .'

Cassie said, 'Put on some music, maybe the artist formerly known as Prince for the guy who used to have hair . . . how would that be.'

I said, 'Everybody stay put – and you fuckface, wot's yer real name.'

'Believe it or not, it's David. Is that serendipity or what?'

'You knew I couldn't understand how Cassie could

follow me so successfully . . . but, if she'd a partner . . . What I can't get is why.'

Cassie shrugged, 'Bucks – as mundane as that.'

Letterman smiled, said, 'You've gotta admit, you're a natural patsy, the original fall guy.'

I used the gun to indicate the room, asked, 'But this place, the Audi . . .'

'All hired.'

'And are ye . . . related?'

Letterman gave a snigger, 'Only in the sack buddy.'

Cassie began a series of stretches, said, 'What are you gonna do now hot-shot. I mean, you have a plan . . . right.'

Letterman added, 'No shit buddy but first, I did give the straight gen on one thing . . . I was in the Marine Corps and they *showed us . . .*'

He did some split-second manoeuvre, his leg shot out nd my gun went flying across the room

'. . . *this* . . .'

With a second kick to my chest I was thrown back across a sofa to curl on the floor in agony.

'. . . and *that* . . . impressive huh!'

Cassie retrieved the gun and examined it closely. Letterman hunkered down in front of me, said, 'See this hand, not a fist . . . watch the birdy.'

Shot it into my chest. The pain was nothing I'd ever experienced, it burned screaming into my brain. I couldn't help it and roared, he roared right along with me. When I stopped he said, 'I guess you won't tell where the loot is but I've got a few methods to change your mind. Lemme give you a pointer, it involves a needle.'

Believed him, said, 'I'll tell you.'

And did.

My body was paralysed. I couldn't move to even relocate the pain. Letterman said to Cassie, 'You wanna do him sugar?'

'Why bother, just leave him.'

'Hey babe, he'd come after us . . . motherfucker doesn't know how to quit.'

'We could drop a dime on him, let the cops have his ass.'

'Naw, he'd give us up.'

He bounced upright and left the room. My eyes locked on Cassie's, hers had an expression of . . . such softness, it was eerie. I asked her, 'Did you burn my house?'

'Yes.'

'Why?'

'To get your attention.'

Back he came with a kitchen knife, saying, 'This fucker's not even sharp but, what the hell.'

Cassie said, 'Let's not do this.'

'Get real babe, he's a liability.'

And bent down whisperin', 'Thing about a blade is . . . it's so personal, goddamn intimate. Am I gettin' hot already . . . Cassie . . . I'm gonna need my ashes hauled.'

The shot was loud in the room and a coin-sized hole appeared above his left eye. Then he fell beside me. Cassie said, 'We're pulling the plug on your show, the ratings just aren't there.'

Again I tried to move but the effort was awesome, she said, 'If you lie very still for a time, gradually the agony will slip away.'

'How the fuck would you know.'

'He's done it to me.'

She began to collect her things and then rummaged in my clothes, found a key to my room. So close I could have kissed her. Then she laid her hand on my bald skull, said, 'I prefer you with hair.'

And she stood up, ready to leave. I shouted, 'You want me to thank you for saving me . . . is that it?'

'No David, I guess I don't.'

'At least tell me what the fuck all of this was for . . . Did you kill Laura . . . Why'd you shoot Doc! Who the bloody hell are you?'

She smiled and answered, 'I'm no big deal.'

'Wait . . . I mean . . . c'mon . . . was anything true . . . your bone disease, the daughter?'

'In Morocco they say the only truth is the love of a child. But hey, maybe that's a crock.'

Then she was gone. As she'd said, the pain began to fade but it was still two hours before I could move sufficiently to get out of there. I stood for a moment over Letterman and said, 'Not so hot now eh!'

By the time I got to The Gate, Cassie had three hours on me. How long would it take to walk away with a million quid.

The house was quiet and I had to force the door. I hoped she hadn't shot the landlady.

The suitcase was on the bed, a white envelope resting on it. I opened the case, the money was gone. Then I grabbed the envelope, one short sheet, it read:

> '*Guess Who*
> The lady is gone
> who stood in the way so long
> the hypnosis is over
> and no one calls encore
> to the song.'

I sat on the bed and tried to see how I'd lost it all,

Doc
Cassie
The money
ME.

Yeah, when those blasts took the cashier, they took me too. I hadn't been caught but, oh shit, I hadn't got away. What is it – the bank robbers' prayer: 'Lemme get away CLEAN.'

I was dirty to my soul and I felt it began to leak, to seep and fester.

Some line of MacNeice . . . to wait for the gun-butt . . . rap upon the door.

I began my sentence, this was hard time all the way.

On the floor I saw a pack of Camel Lights and, way-to-go, a battered Zippo.

Thinking 'Why the hell not?' I shook one free, got it in my mouth and cranked the Zippo, one, two, three.

Zip

Nada

Zilch

Outa gas.